COURTING IN CUSTER

SEVEN BRIDES OF SOUTH DAKOTA: BOOK 7

KARI TRUMBO

ISBN- 10: 0-9987309-9-8

I SBN-13: 978-0-9987309-9-8

Courting in Custer

© 2018 Kari Trumbo

Published by Kari Trumbo, All Rights Reserved

Scripture quotations are from the King James Version of the Bible

Author's note: This is a work of fiction. All locations, characters, names, and actions are a product of the author's overactive imagination. Any resemblance, however subtle, to living persons or actual places and events are coincidental.

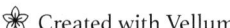 Created with Vellum

CHAPTER 1

Custer, South Dakota June 1909

I f only something would happen so that every day wasn't just like the last. Daisy let her mind wander during a break between cases at the Custer County Courthouse. She'd earned the job of court reporter because of her attention to detail and her ability to remain completely silent, though it wasn't difficult on days like this where she was bored to tears. Her instructors had found her silence odd; however, coming from a small house with seven sisters that were forever talking *for* her, Daisy just never piped up unless it was called for, because she didn't need to.

"All rise," the bailiff's voice broke above the murmurs throughout the room. The deep cherry wood furniture gleamed in the morning light through the tall leaded windows. "The State versus Saunders."

She never had to stand. She had to be ready in case anything happened, though it never did. Her hands were forever poised and ready to record the action in quick shorthand on her steno machine. While the defendant and his lawyer came up front, another man slipped into the back of the room followed by a lawyer, who couldn't hide if he wanted to, through the narrowly opened double door. The broad shoulders were strangely familiar, and she did her best to hold in her gasp and continue to pay attention. As he turned, her stomach did a sweet flip. His face had matured much in the six years since she'd last seen him, but she would never forget the man, or the pact she'd made with him.

Everyone sat, and her fingers quivered over the keys. Would he see her and recognize her as she had him? Daisy closed her eyes for a moment, focused. She couldn't let him distract her. But why was he there? The judge would speak soon, and she'd have to pay close attention. Though, with shorthand, it was much easier to keep up. Her wits had to be firmly in place, even for the brief citations that were common in the small courtroom. She was able to type at almost three hundred words per minute if she had to, but it wasn't expressly necessary in her current job.

Within minutes, the proceedings had finished, and Judge Cornwall called the bailiff forward. The uniformed man turned to the courtroom and addressed everyone.

"This court will take a short recess. Mr. Laury, please join Judge Cornwall in his chambers."

Mr. Laury, though Daisy had known him as Elias his

whole life, caught her eye for a but a moment as he strode by. He'd always been a tall man with broad, strong shoulders and intelligent brown eyes. Now, a well-trimmed beard adorned his jaw. He didn't smile at her, he never really had, but she could see the warmth of recognition there.

Daisy laid her hands in her lap and tried to keep from fidgeting. The heat of Elias's gaze left her the moment he passed her seat as he went back into chambers. Judge Cornwall hated fidgeting, especially in women, but it was so difficult to keep still when her heart was pounding so. It would be at least fifteen minutes until they returned, and the court was soon full of soft chatter and people moving about to either leave or visit with those nearby.

In her last year of high school, back in 1903, she and Elias had been as close of friends as either of them had ever had. She had been the quiet type, the one who avoided talking to everyone. She often sat at the base of the tree outside the school and waited for her brother-in-law, Beau, to pick her up, knowing the tree would be quiet and no one would bother her. Well, no one but him. Elias had no trouble speaking up in class when it was needed, but kept to himself otherwise. He often joined her under the maple tree. Sometimes they would talk, other times they'd just study.

On one spring day, right before graduation, he'd come out and sat with her, pulled out his book and flipped it open, then cleared his throat.

"Daisy?" he'd whispered to get her attention, not that

she'd been able to focus much once he sat down.

"Yes?" She held her finger to her spot, so he wouldn't realize he'd distracted her well before he'd said anything.

"Have you ever been kissed?" His ears tinged red and he kept his nose in his book, though she could now see he held it upside down.

"No, have you?" Her breath stalled in her chest and she prayed he hadn't. Would this be the moment she'd been dreaming of? Was this the moment Elias finally took notice of her? Though he'd never so much as smiled at her, when he spoke to her, she felt special, like she mattered to someone. He made her feel as if he *wanted* to hear her voice, even if it was only once in a while.

"Lands, no. Like any girl would want to kiss me." He laughed nervously, fumbling with his book.

She wanted to pipe up that *she* would, but her embarrassment kept her silent. He'd never asked her such an intimate question and probably wasn't really looking for an answer. Usually, he wanted to talk politics or literature, safe topics, since they both agreed with one another.

"Daisy, I don't see myself getting married. I just can't seem to talk to women."

"Well, you seem to talk to me just fine." His nervousness had heat rushing up her own neck.

If the handsome and well-spoken Elias Laury was going to be alone, she probably would, as well. Who wanted a soft-spoken, plain little mouse when they could have someone pretty and perfect? Even her sisters were all prettier, more accomplished, than she. And every last one of them was married, two of them when they were as old as she was just then.

He took a deep breath. "You're not the same."

He wasn't going to kiss her. He was only there to make conversation, yet again. This time on the politics of future romance...that she would never have.

"I don't think I'll get married, either, Elias. There's no shame in being alone." Though she didn't quite believe that; the tension humming through her claimed she was lying to him. Every last one of her beautiful sisters was married to a man that made their hearts sing. But, no man had ever shown her the least bit of interest and, unlike all her sisters, she didn't go anywhere or have any sort of adventure planned where she would meet such a man. Elias would be leaving for Harvard within the month, so even the one man who *had* spoken to her would be gone.

"Promise me something, Daisy?" He'd slid a little closer to her, brushing her shoulder with his broad one. He turned, looking her full in the eyes, his so wide and a warm brown that wasn't quite like anyone else. "Promise me that if we both make it to our twenty-fifth birthday and haven't wed, we'll marry each other. That way, we won't be alone."

He pulled a sheet of paper from the back of his book, and on it he had written it out—like a contract—for both of them to sign. She'd marry Elias right there under that tree if he'd asked her, but waiting seven years wouldn't be *so* long.

That long-ago promise, signed and sealed under that

tree, seemed frivolous and silly in the light of the court-room setting now. He'd been going away to law school and she thought he'd never come back, at least, she hadn't thought he'd come back alone.

After a year of sitting out at the ranch in Deadwood, she'd sent off to various places, found a temporary job in Deadwood, and then finally settled on learning how to use the stenography machine in the courthouse. She'd applied to many positions, but she'd gotten the one in Custer. It was just an hour away from her sister, Nora, in Hot Springs.

The judges chamber door opened, and Elias's client looked fit to burst as he staggered out. He was agitated and Elias had a hold of his arm to steady him. The bailiff excused everyone in the court for the day, making the announcement of when court would open the following day. Though she hadn't been in chambers for the confer-ence, she would be given notes to add to the case file. That would be her work to do back in her small, cramped office, where she spent hours after court, retyping all of the short-hand into regular pages of notes. Some would call it tedious, but it was constant, and she had nowhere else to be, anyway.

Elias again caught her glance and raised his chin slightly in greeting. His eyes crinkled, yet he didn't smile. Would he want to see her? Where had he been for the last seven years? And, why had he suddenly shown up in *her* courtroom? The way his gaze bore into her, as if he was memorizing every inch of her, made her believe he wasn't married. Though, it wouldn't matter. He probably didn't even remember that pact they'd made so long ago. They weren't children anymore, and it made no sense to keep silly promises. Though, the way her nerves thrummed as he looked at her, her head was having little effect over her heart.

Elias spoke to his client at the table assigned to the defense. Prosecution had returned to judge's chambers with the judge, but Daisy couldn't quiet bring herself to care. Thankfully, she wouldn't be called upon to concentrate the rest of the day, because her thoughts couldn't be controlled, and neither could her fidgeting as she waited for the court to clear. The bailiff strode by her and took Elias's client into custody. It didn't mean he was guilty, just that they didn't want him to run. He'd probably get his day in court very soon, which meant more days with Elias close by.

She wanted to pack up her little stenography machine and run before Elias could come to the front and talk to her. It would mean she could keep on dreaming about why he was there, instead of what was most-likely a boring reality. He wanted to speak to her, even now he kept catching her gaze, but it could be that he merely recognized her and wanted to greet her. Could they still have anything to talk about after so long? Dare she hold on to hope?

"Daisy?" The same tentative voice from so many years before interrupted her thoughts.

"Elias." She turned to face him and was struck again by his height. She would have to stand on the tips of her toes to kiss him. Heat flushed her cheeks. Where had *that* thought come from?

"It's been a long time." His soft voice had gotten deeper, more confident. It was that of a man now, not a boy making senseless promises under a tree.

"It has. What brings you to Custer?" She tried to sound light, but her throat was suddenly too dry. She carefully rolled the scroll of steno paper so that she only had to glance at him periodically. She didn't trust herself to look directly in his eyes.

He laughed a moment and fidgeted with his tie. "Actually...*you*. I turned twenty-five three months ago. I was waiting until your birthday to see if you'd managed to find a husband yet."

Daisy gasped as she did a quick tally in her head. Yes, he would've had his birthday in February, hers was in a few days.

"You came all the way back to Custer from Massachusetts to see if I'd married?" She wanted to laugh, it seemed so absurd, but if he'd really come all that way, then he was serious. "If I'd known, I would've just sent you a letter."

"A letter wouldn't have mattered. I really needed to be here for this, and I already checked in the record, so I know you're not." His voice dropped subtly and some of his confidence melted away. "Are you still spending your evenings reading under trees?" He leaned against the judge's high bench, glancing down at her with those same warm brown eyes she'd been dreaming about for years.

8

He *did* remember. She closed her eyes and pictured her favorite spot. Yes, every evening she buried her head in one of the books her sister Frances wrote, and prayed that someday, someone would find her beautiful or exciting. All the women in her sister's books were lovely and had grand adventures. If only she could have an exploit or two, and a husband who loved her to distraction... But a meaningless infatuation with a boy from school couldn't turn into love, even when the boy had become such a handsome, accomplished man. She had but to look up into his eyes to see that. It wasn't love in them, merely curiosity, and how could it be anything else? They were strangers now.

"I still enjoy reading, yes."

Elias pulled a slip of paper from his pocket and handed it to her. He had yet to smile and it made her nervous. She took it from him and flipped it open, then gasped. It was a court summons at 8AM on her birthday.

"What is this about?" Terror ripped through her and she dug for her kerchief in her pocket to dab at her temples. Had she witnessed some type of crime and not realized it?

"It's your wedding, Daisy. I'm sure you'll be lovely. Happy birthday." His eyes warmed to a deep chocolate as he turned and grabbed his hat off the desk, tipped it onto his head, and left the courthouse. Daisy's knees shook as she took one more look at the paper.

Her wedding?

CHAPTER 2

Seven long years he'd thought about Daisy every single day. As he walked home from the courthouse, he couldn't help but think about his past. So many things had to happen so he could have his moment with Daisy in court. Each exam, he'd told himself he was that much closer, and every birthday he'd made another mental tally mark on the calendar. Now, he was there, and everything was as it should be. Daisy was still waiting for him.

He'd also done a lot of praying, praying that he'd grown to hate himself for, as it was selfish. He'd prayed that his beloved Daisy wouldn't be married, that she wouldn't even meet anyone, while he was gone. He didn't want her to have to compare him to anyone else and find him lacking. No man should pray for the woman he loved to be lonely, but he'd done it.

He'd had to do as his parents wished: go to Harvard,

learn what he needed to pass his exams. Then, when he'd done all that they'd required of him, he came back, knowing he could provide for Daisy. She would appreciate that he could take care of her because she would want for nothing.

She'd never want him, tall as he was, so he'd had to use his wits to get her to agree. Though it had seemed under-handed, it was his only chance. She had been too perfect to let slip away, and she still was. Some man would've scooped her up if he hadn't planted that little seed, his contract for a marriage, so long ago. He'd wanted her to believe she could forget about looking, forget about trying to find a companion, because he would always be there, even when he *hadn't* been. And it had worked. Daisy was alone, but not for long.

His heart had wanted to leap right out of his chest when he'd walked into that courtroom and saw her soft golden curls tucked around her perfect face and flush cheeks, her lush pink lips parted in surprise. Now, his prayer had to change. The Lord had kept her for him, but now, he'd need help the Lord's help to court his bride. After he wed her. But only enough to keep her happy with him. They both would have to learn to love from opposite ends of the house. Daisy was too perfect to ever touch.

The court case before his client's had been short, but he'd used every minute to watch her, her tiny fingers had moved deftly over the keys. Daisy had always been adept at whatever she'd decided to do. That had kept him through the years *and* terrified him. If she'd set her mind to finding a husband, she'd be married, and there wouldn't have been a thing he could do about it.

He wasn't handsome, according to his mother, not as strong in the arms as the ranchers Daisy was used to seeing, nor was he spindly as many men of the age were. He'd been tall his whole life and most women he'd met wanted nothing to do with him, save Daisy. She'd always made time for him, talked to him, smiled at him. Their conversations had been pleasant, satisfying, addicting. He could talk about anything from faith to law, and she would speak her mind, never implying that her ideas were better or worse. And he adored her wit and intelligence. Frankly, he'd treasured every part of her, and that hadn't lessened in his absence.

Now that he'd left the courtroom and he'd given her the *summons* the judge had helped him arrange, he couldn't settle his stomach. Seven long years of waiting, hoping, praying, and all of it could be dashed if she didn't show up. They had signed that slip of paper he'd prepared, when he'd asked her so long ago under that tree. He'd kept that paper in his Bible, but it was worthless. As a lawyer, he knew that. She probably knew that, too, since she was now familiar with the court system. At the time, before he'd studied much of anything, he'd thought her signature made his plan foolproof. The only loophole had been if she had chosen someone else. *He'd* certainly never planned to find anyone, there was no one but Daisy. But the only fool had been him, she could walk away from him at any moment.

It was possible she was, even now, thinking of some way out. All she needed to do was hand him the biggest embarrassment of his life, which was to be left at the altar in the court he'd made his second home.

His own home came into view as he walked down Third Street. It was small, purchased just the week before when he'd arrived back in Custer after studying and building a practice in Massachusetts. But neither the east, nor his new house, felt like home. He finished walking to his modest story and a half house and pushed open the door. His little liver and white spaniel bounded down the stairs to meet him.

"Gracie, girl." He ruffled her ears. She was an exceptional bird dog and he'd finally get the chance to hunt with her, now that he was back in Dakota. All he had to do was drive east river—as the locals called it—and the prairie had more birds than a man could ever hunt. He let the dog outside and slipped his hat onto the lone hook by the door. He stared at it for a moment and warmth spread through his chest. He'd have to put up a second hook in the next few days, along with a few other things to get his house ready to finally be a home, with a wife. *Daisy.*

He'd need to buy a new dresser for her, so she had somewhere to keep her clothes. He'd need more linens for the bathroom. As he wandered through the house, listing the various items he'd need, he stopped short outside of his bedroom. Every man wanted intimacy with his bride, but Daisy wouldn't be a typical bride, and theirs wouldn't be a typical relationship. Even if she eventually wanted him physically, he wouldn't allow it. For her sake, they could never lay together. At least she would be with him always. He'd never have to be alone, and neither would she since he'd never leave her.

Gracie whined at the door and he made his way back through the house to let her in. He opened the door to find a man in a high-button dark suit from the Fitch & Willis general store striding up his walk. Elias recognized him from the week before when he'd picked up a few groceries. The man's face scrunched as he stared at the house number.

"Can I help you?" Elias opened the door all the way and held it for him.

The man stopped and squinted. "You Elias Laury?"

Elias couldn't help but feel annoyed, the man was interrupting him, and he had only a few days. "Yes. What can I do for you?"

The man finally smiled and handed him a small box. "We don't normally deliver, but the little lady had such a nice smile. You take care now." The man tipped his hat and turned, quickly heading back toward town.

The little lady?

He looked at the plain brown card stock box. Who would be sending him anything, and why bother? He didn't even know anyone in Custer except…

Could it be?

He made sure Gracie was in, then closed the door, locking it behind him. The box was light but so were his feet as he rushed for the kitchen. He opened the box, and inside was a small cake with frosting, and a note.

Elias,

I'm sorry I missed your birthday, especially when you went to such great lengths for mine. Perhaps, if we are to go through with this, we should take the next few days to reacquaint ourselves? I will wait by the First National Bank at six this evening. If I don't see you, I'll know that you are as nervous as I am about this. But I do hope I'll not be waiting long.

Yours in time,

Daisy Arnsby

He couldn't breathe. Daisy wanted to talk with him. The sweet, quiet young woman had found her voice, at least a little, and she had more gumption than he'd given her credit for. If it were possible, he loved her even more for her found pluck. He took the little cake and hid it up in the cupboard so Gracie couldn't get at it.

He couldn't help but smile as he loosened his tie. "I'm going to the bank tonight, girl. You'll be good, won't you?"

She cocked her head to the side and stared at him. Even when they'd traveled by train, she'd been a good companion. Always with him, always happy to see him. She would be thrown off when he left in the evening, and even more so when he brought Daisy there to his home in just a few days.

He knelt in front of the dog and gently scratched her

neck. The dog was a great companion, but she wouldn't compare to Daisy. "It won't be long now, girl. Then we won't be alone."

She nosed under his chin, leaving a chilly trail, and he patted her head, then stood. He had to get some supper for him and Gracie before getting ready to go back downtown. There was so much to do before he had to leave to make it there in time.

He'd never been so worried about how he looked for such a simple trip. There was nothing he could do to make himself look like other men, he'd tried. So, hopefully she could learn to be happy with a man who filled a room. He stood in his kitchen and realized his joking thought was true, he did fill the room. He could reach from one end of it to the other if he wanted to. Gracie barked to remind him to hurry as he put some meat and gravy in her dish.

"I know you're happy with me, girl. And maybe someday, Daisy will be, too."

CHAPTER 3

Daisy stared at the little paper with the date and time of her birthday wedding on it. She sat in her small room at the boarding house, within view of the bank, and wondered what Elias would think of the little cake she'd had the grocer deliver. Years ago, he'd liked sweet treats, but so many years could change anyone. Patches, her tiny red tabby, jumped onto her lap and purred as she settled in.

She would never admit to anyone that Patches was such a dear friend to her, but who else could she talk to? Even those who wanted to be alone needed someone occasionally. The cat never complained and seemed to like her company just as much, no matter if she conversed with her or was silent. Patches wouldn't finish her sentences, nor would she make decisions for Daisy like her sisters had. She just listened, and that was exactly the friend Daisy needed. Not to mention, Patches kept the mice away.

"If I do this, I'll never have grand adventures like the heroines in Frances's books. I'll never find that someone who loves me so much his eyes soften in the moonlight and his kiss makes my knees weak." She sighed and slid her hand down the length of Patches' back. "Elias didn't even kiss me when he had the chance. Though, maybe he never really wanted to. He might still never want to."

She stroked the cat, but it didn't calm her as it usually did. "I've always liked him, but he's not adventuresome, nor does he particularly like me. He never spoke to me overmuch. The only reason he chose *me* to make that pact was because I was the least likely to be married by the age of twenty-five. Even back then, he knew that, of all the others to pick from, I was the one sure to be alone." Daisy sighed as her shoulders fell along with her thoughts, and Patches stared up at her, waiting for more attention. When she didn't move to pet the cat, Patches stood and pressed her head to Daisy's chin until she relented and resumed her petting.

"Part of me is really sad, Patches. If I do this, it will make me unhappy every time I'm with my family because my sisters all have what I wanted. But maybe that's just plain selfish. The Lord doesn't want us to compare our blessings to others. I've always adored that man, but I'd also wanted someone who adored me right back. Maybe that was too much to ask for? I should be happy that any man at all wants such a mousy, old woman who doesn't talk to anyone but her cat. If someone was going to come and sweep me off my feet, he'd have done it by now."

Patches heaved an indignant sound in her throat and jumped off Daisy's lap as the clock struck five. Only one hour to eat, if she could, and then go down and wait to see if Elias would meet her. Her hands shook slightly as she opened a can of beans for her dinner. She rarely cooked anything that wasn't canned, since it was just herself and food was expensive on her small salary. Most of her canned meals often stretched into two, for the sake of her budget.

After picking at her supper for a few minutes, her stomach churning with nerves, she found she wouldn't be able to eat until the evening was over and she could be done with it. Elias might not even come, and what would they talk about if he did? She knew nothing about him other than he'd been in Massachusetts at law school. She'd done no traveling other than from Deadwood, where her family still lived, to Custer for her job. He was well-traveled in comparison. Elias would find her dull, most everyone did.

Daisy ducked quietly down the hall outside her room to avoid disturbing any of her neighbors as she inched down the squeaky stairwell. Mrs. Bates didn't like to be disturbed during her supper, and Mr. Natchez suffered from headaches. One minor groan of a stair tread could cause either of them discomfort. Once outside, she turned her face up to the sun and let it warm her for a moment. Everything would be all right. She would be fine. A husband would mean she wouldn't have to worry about her food budget. She would share the load with someone else. If he didn't love her, well, it wasn't about love. It never had been. Elias had wisely decided that being alone was a bad way to go through life and he'd ensured that neither of them would. It was noble. Just not the slightest bit romantic. Yet, why crave outside of her needs? The Lord had provided a man, a wonderful man, to provide for her. Putting aside her craving for adventure and romance was an easy idea, but in practice, would be one of the hardest things she'd ever done.

Though she'd hoped he would be there early, the front of the bank was empty. It was tempting to go inside and see the pretty interior, but then she might miss Elias. It was close enough to six that if she was inside, she might miss seeing him. If he didn't show up, she would dash into Fitch and Willis's for something to do that evening to keep her mind off of why he might not want to spend time with her.

Her sister, Eva, was both an artist and a reader. She had worked with the city of Lead to create a public library donated by Phoebe Hearst. And now, they were working toward building an opera house for the town. Daisy was still waiting for Custer to get a library.

Fifteen years after Eva and her dear George met at the Lead library, they had three rambunctious boys and a precious, though quiet, little girl who couldn't walk down the street without her brothers protecting her the whole way. But they still loved to visit the library.

It was difficult to wait, and not appear like she was waiting. The bank was a narrow, large brick building. If she'd thought ahead, she would've asked to meet him somewhere farther down the street where there were benches on the boardwalk. People walked by and stared, nodding slightly as they passed, and Elias still didn't come. Daisy pulled her little time piece from her pocket and opened the front. He was only a few minutes late. It was possible he'd been detained, or he hadn't gotten the message. She'd had to ask the judge for Elias's address, then rush to the store for the cake. The grocer hadn't been certain when he would be able to deliver it, though, she'd asked for it to go right away.

The sun warmed her head and face and she tried to enjoy herself, though she'd rather be sitting at home with Patches than be out and about, forced to nod and smile at everyone. She searched the street once more and a broad-shouldered, tall man ambled toward her. Something within her fluttered to life. It had to be Elias, no other man was quite the same. At least to her. As he got closer, she could see he'd taken off his suit coat and tie from earlier, but still wore his crisp white shirt and well-cut black trousers. I was obvious that Elias didn't get his clothes second hand.

As his eyes lit upon her, his face softened with recognition. He'd never done that before, and it changed his whole face. Was it possible that he was looking forward to meeting with her as much as she was with him? He strode up to her, his old confidence in place.

"Good evening, Daisy."

There was no need for formality, they had known each

other since grade school, proper names would've been stuffy, odd, uncomfortable.

"Good evening, Elias." She smiled and wished he'd do the same. "Where would you like to go to sit and talk for a while?"

He laughed for a moment before he caught himself and she wished he hadn't. His laughter was a window into the real man, the man she'd never seen before, but would soon be married to.

"I'm afraid I don't know much about the city. I just moved here, and I've spent most of that time finding a place to live and getting a few cases going."

Her most favorite place was a small park down by French Creek. It had a few benches and it wasn't far. It reminded her of the school yard where Elias had visited her under the tree and proposed—if she could even call it that. "I have a suggestion, if you don't mind staying outside?"

He offered his elbow. "Lead the way."

His arm was strong under her fingertips even through the thin cotton of his shirt. As they walked, she tried to recall all the things she'd wanted to learn about him, but now that he was right there, she found it difficult to think of anything. Where could she start? He wouldn't be anything like the boy she'd known.

"So," he ventured, "what made you decide to go into court reporting? That is a fairly new profession, at least for women."

That was a long story, and she didn't want to bore him

with details of her own life. She'd taken the long way around the barn when it had come to making a living, after realizing she wouldn't be able just marry and have a family like many other women her age.

"I started out taking a typing course for journalism. I had planned to join my brother-in-law, Clive, in Deadwood at the newspaper. When I finished, the state was pulling out of a recession and there were no jobs. I worked for a while in a law office as a secretary, and the lawyer suggested I take a course in shorthand and stenography. He thought I would be good at it. Not to mention, he didn't need me anymore, but felt guilty about letting me go." She still chaffed at the memory. After that, she'd refused to work for anyone who might become a friend. It had hurt him financially to keep her as long as he did. She didn't want to be a financial burden on anyone.

"You always did have a fine attention to detail." He stared ahead, but his compliment sent warmth right to her heart. No one ever noticed *anything* about her.

"Thank you. I see you went ahead with your parents' plan and attended Harvard. They must be incredibly proud of you."

Elias waited to answer, as if he needed to mull everything over for its value before he spoke. "Yes, it turned out they were right. It was a profession I was well-suited to and leaves me in the unique position of being able to work anywhere I choose."

As they reached the little park, Daisy stopped leading them and let Elias pick where he'd like to take them. She held her breath as they approached the bench where she usually sat to read, right under a large silver maple tree. Custer had very few trees. It was situated in a wide grassy valley. That made the little tree all the more special to her. When he stopped there, at her spot, and motioned for her to sit, it was like a little whisper from Heaven that things would change, but they didn't have to change completely. Elias would fit into her life, if she just let him.

CHAPTER 4

E lias felt the change in Daisy the moment she started following his steps, instead of choosing her own. She loosened her stride, like they were dancing together. It was momentous to him, a changing of the guard, symbolic of what he'd hoped to achieve. She wanted *him* to guide her to a place, to lead her.

After a minute of looking, he chose a bench with a pretty tree that reminded him of the one where he'd proposed, if he could be so bold as to call it that. Daisy sat down, her skirt rustling softly. She was so poised. Everything about her was tiny compared to him, and it worried him. Would she fear him when they were alone?

He'd never forget a comment his grandmother had made in passing, when she'd thought he couldn't hear: '*It's really too bad he's such a big fellow. Life will be hard for him alone. Women will be plum terrified...*' The words, and the assumption that his size would mean he'd never find love, had stayed with him even now. Reoccurring instances throughout his days had only underscored his fear. He was just too big to love.

His grandmother had professed to love him, she'd never say anything to purposely hurt him, nor would she whisper an untruth. Her words had been part of why he'd asked Daisy to sign his contract and make that pact with him so long ago. He would never find someone to love him, but he didn't want to be alone. However, if he ever went too far, tried to be with her as a husband, he might hurt her, and he'd never forgive himself for that. He wouldn't let himself get any closer to her than a faithful companion.

Daisy glanced at him out of the corner of her eye and held her hands together in her lap. The slight breezed fluttered the ruffle around her narrow shoulders. He wanted to reach over and weave her small fingers with his own, to feel what it would be like to protect even just that little bit of her. Was her skin soft? Her hair? He didn't know. He'd never held a woman's hand, nor anything else.

He had to find out more about her and her past. Was she still the woman he remembered? "You took the class to be a court reporter. What made you choose Custer and not Deadwood? Deadwood has a fairly active court."

She tucked her head sweetly, and her voice was as soft as evening birdsong. "I tried. I applied for positions within an hour of home, but Custer was the place that answered and hired me. I'm thankful to have a job at all. So many women are struggling to find employment now, before they wed... It's difficult to find a position for those of us who didn't plan to *ever* be wed." She gasped and covered her lips, her eyes wide and pleading for forgiveness. "I'm sorry. I shouldn't have said that."

His heart plummeted, but, of course it was true. She would've assumed he'd gone off to Massachusetts and that absolved her of her silly agreement, one she wouldn't have made if he hadn't made her feel like she would be alone otherwise. Even with his guilt, he couldn't let her go. If he did, he'd never convince her to marry him without the pact. Why would she ever want to?

"Did you think I would forget about our agreement?" His training as a lawyer took over, and he steeled his voice against the hurt he didn't want to feel.

"No." She blushed. "I assumed you would wed the first pretty, intelligent woman you met, and forget all about someone like me. It wasn't like you couldn't."

Could she really believe that? He wanted to think so, that she would believe so highly of him, to find him capable of finding love from someone else. But it just wasn't possible. Even if it *had* been, he'd never tried. Daisy and her pretty smile and witty conversation had his heart from the first. He couldn't even look at another woman without comparing her to Daisy, and they'd all fallen sorely short.

"I'm afraid there was no one else. Didn't *you* ever look? We've been out of school now for a long time. You had plenty of opportunity, and if you were working, you must have met an abundance of men." Though he'd hoped she hadn't.

She laughed, short and dry, almost forced. "I don't meet men. I go to work and come home. I shop when I need something from the store, otherwise, it's just me and my cat."

That surprised him. He'd never thought of Daisy needing anyone. "You have a cat?" It bothered him to know that she had been as lonely as he'd been before he'd gotten Gracie. His faithful dog had never had to live with another pet, and if her cat was half as close to her as he was with Gracie, he couldn't ask her to give it up. Though, he'd never much liked the wily things.

"Yes, she's been with me for quite a few years. I'm a bit embarrassed to say that she keeps me company. I don't talk much with other people. My work requires me to be quiet, I guess I've fallen into a habit."

He had to hold himself back from taking her hand now. Would she welcome the small comfort? "You don't need to be embarrassed, but how do you think she'll handle living with a dog?"

A pretty blush crept up her cheeks. "I guess we'll find out soon enough. Did you like your cake?"

He'd forgotten to thank her, what an ungrateful lout. "It was perfect, thank you."

"I didn't think, until after I'd sent it, that perhaps you don't like sweets anymore."

Did she remember *everything* about him? He hadn't gotten anything for himself in so long, maybe he didn't, but he wasn't about to tell her that. Not when she was the only one who'd even thought about his birthday in years.

"It was thoughtful of you, and I appreciate it, but let's talk for a minute about your birthday. It's coming soon."

Her eyes met his for a moment and they were exactly as he remembered, almost lavender, simply lovely, like no other gem on earth. She had the most unique eyes he'd ever seen and, though they were beautiful, they were just one of the things he loved about her. It was her whole face and manner that enchanted him, not just one piece. For any one part was pretty on its own, but as a whole, she set his heart to beating faster than the waltz.

"My birthday hasn't been cause to celebrate for many years," she mumbled.

"Well, I should say it will be this year. Is there anything you need beforehand?" He had to assume that she would go through with the wedding. If he didn't, she would discover just how nervous he was that she would walk away.

"Am I to invite my family to come, or…" Her voice stalled.

He had to let her know that he didn't expect her to love him, and their marriage didn't have to be real beyond the legal sense. She could let go of that worry he could see building in the furrows of her forehead. Neither of them would be alone, but they would also never be together. She didn't have to worry about her giant husband taking advantage of her.

"I don't think it's necessary. You can ask them if you

think they would like to be there, or if they will be offended if you don't. But our marriage will be, as we agreed to, one of convenience. So that neither of us have to face the strife and struggle of loneliness."

She sat silently for a moment and her eyes turned glassy as she blinked quickly. Her lip trembled slightly, and she slid down the bench from him a few inches. He reached to pull her back, but her flinch made him stop. Would he lose her the very day he'd finally talked to her again?

Her voice creaked when she was finally able to make it work. "If you don't really want to wed, then why did you come back here? I see no reason to go so far out of your way for something you'd rather not do." She closed her eyes as glistening tears appeared at the edges, then she stared over her shoulder, blocking his view of her face.

Those tears tore at his already aching heart. "I told you, there were no other women, and I don't want to be by myself. That's why I made the pact with you in the first place." He hoped she would turn and look at him, to relax and understand that he didn't expect her to ever love him, that things would be just as they had always been for her, only now she would have the support of one who loved her.

Instead, she hunkered into herself and turned her knees farther from him. "I don't require anything in the next few days. However, I hope you recall that *you* have a little more than one whole day to change your mind or find someone else entirely."

Her words gutted him. There would never be anyone else. She stood and made to walk away.

"Daisy, wait!" He stood and followed her. She kept walking but slowed her pace, not that it mattered, he would've caught up quickly with his long legs. "Let me walk you back to the bank, at least."

"I don't think that's necessary." Her words were as stiff as her spine. She wouldn't look at him and he wanted to tip her face up to his, to understand what she was hiding from him. They had started out so well.

"If you think your family would want to know, I welcome them." He strode alongside her, but she didn't stop.

"That's fine. If this is nothing more than a contractual relationship, I won't burden them with it." Her tone crackled like broken glass.

"I don't foresee our relationship being a burden to anyone, Daisy. I hope you don't see it that way." He had to find something to say to stop her, so he could talk to her and find out what he'd said or done.

"How else should I see it? You've shown up, a well-to-do lawyer who's come to rescue poor Daisy Arnsby who couldn't manage to find a real husband of her own. But don't worry, it's not like you'll have to *really* play husband, either. It's all for show." She wrapped her arms around her stomach and picked up her pace.

"Daisy, I didn't mean to hurt you. I never assumed that you'd still be alone. In fact, I was quite surprised when I arrived in town and found that you were. I almost missed your birthday, because it took me so long to find you." He had looked for many months, assuming she would've stayed near her family. He'd been so worried that the reason he couldn't find her was that her name had changed.

He'd been too afraid to talk to Beau, though he knew him, because he would've had to explain why he wanted to know where she was. He might have had to ask permission, and Beau might not have given it.

"Well, I didn't. I never planned to get married. I didn't even look. No one wants to marry a quiet little nothing. Not even the man who agreed to years ago. Don't worry about me, Elias. I free you of your obligation. I don't want to strap any man down, and I refuse to be a burden to anyone. I don't want a contractual marriage and I won't force you into a farce, either. Good evening." She dashed off across the street from the bank and he refused to chase after her any further when he was only making her angrier.

What had he done? He'd tried to relieve her of her worry, and instead, he'd hurt her to the point of tears. Daisy needed to be cherished and protected, but she needed to be protected from him most of all. Even his words, the part of him most schooled to be normal, had cut her. He was too big, too much of a brute, for her sweet tenderness. But, oh, how he loved her. He couldn't let her just walk out of his life, not now. After so many years of waiting, when she was right there, he couldn't let her go.

CHAPTER 5

The small courtroom didn't hold all that many people and certainly not enough for Elias to hide his tall frame. He felt like a Clydesdale at a pony show. Even sitting in the farthest row, his broad shoulders took up too much room, people sitting next to him cut glances at him with frowns of disapproval. As successful as he was, those glances never ceased to injure.

After Daisy had left him standing alone in front of the bank the evening before, he'd wanted to do little more than hide. But he deserved it. He'd coerced her into signing that promise long ago, and now he'd have to come to grips with the fact that she might not want to go through with it. She had one full day to walk away. Tomorrow, theirs would be the first case of the day, a quick ceremony back in the judge's chambers, then both of them would have to return to work. Just like any other day.

He'd gotten to court early, so he wouldn't have to try to sneak in between cases. His client wouldn't be back in court for another few days, but he didn't have anything else to do, and sitting there in the same room as Daisy made him feel a little closer to her. It also helped him become acquainted with the old judge and how he ran his cases. Since Custer had only one judge, any case he brought would be before Cornwall.

Daisy carried her steno machine in its case and set it on the small desk to the left of the judge's bench. She was so small, with her pristine white shirt and dark green skirt, showing her tiny heeled boots below her hems. No one else even seemed to notice her silent entrance. Her hair was tied back in a perfect bun at her nape, not a wisp of hair out of place. He couldn't help but wonder if she'd stayed up late into the night, or even all night as he had, thinking about their talk in the park and where it had gone wrong.

The only conclusion he could come to was that she was unhappy about a marriage in name only. While that prospect was exciting, it also meant that she couldn't continue on with him at all, because he wouldn't have it any other way. It was the one thing he would be ruthlessly stubborn about. Even if she wanted a relationship with him, he wouldn't allow it. At his size, he'd crush his sweet little flower, and he'd vowed to never hurt her again. He'd done too much of that the night before.

She tucked her skirt close as she sat gracefully and waited for the judge and bailiff. She was early, just as she'd always been when they were at school. Daisy was never late for anything, at least not that he'd ever seen. It wasn't that she enjoyed being early, she just liked to find the place in any situation where she felt the most at ease and stayed there. Her quiet nature had made grade school classmates think she wasn't interested in friendship, when in truth, she was incredibly friendly. Daisy just didn't like being the first to speak. It was how he'd begun their friendship as children. He'd swallowed all his fear one day, sat with her under her tree, and talked to her. She had been so quiet and charming, so ready for anyone to share with her, that he'd made it a point to talk to her whenever he could scrape together enough courage.

The judge strode in from his chambers in his distinguished black suit, and the bailiff announced the start of session. Case after case rolled by as his watch turned ever so slowly. Eight cases later and it was time for recess, so they could have luncheon. If Daisy took a minute to put her equipment together, as she had the day before, he could ask her to join him. Elias waited for a minute, as it was bad form to cross the gates between the courtroom seating and the court itself. Daisy glanced up and saw him. She didn't smile but arranged her roll of paper then came over to the gate.

He met her there. "Daisy, good to see you."

She nodded, her face unchanged. "I didn't expect to see you today. I assumed you would be out looking for some loophole in our agreement."

He'd never heard her so stiff, though she was trying to

portray that she felt nothing, with her chin held high and face blank. He could feel the hurt in her words.

"I don't want to find an escape, do you?" He held his breath and the selfish prayer that had been on his lips for years lifted in his mind once more. *Please, don't let her want anyone else...*

"No, I never said I wanted to break our agreement. I simply don't like the idea of a loveless marriage. We were friends at one time, I think... Is it too much to ask for some smidgen of that once again?" Her bright lavender blue eyes met his and the woman he'd always thought of as meek hit him with pure determination.

He would not agree to anything that would hurt her, but telling her to remain at arm's length already had. "We used to be friends, yes. Does that mean you'll be here tomorrow morning?" He avoided agreeing to anything. She wouldn't force him to lie.

Daisy tilted her head slightly and the sun from the window caught her pretty golden hair. "Yes, I will be here. I'm always here." A slight smile crept over her face. "And will you be here?"

A nervous laugh slipped from him. He'd mostly learned how to control those, but Daisy made him forget everything that was important about being a lawyer. With her, there was only room for what was important to being a man. "I'll be here. Do you want me to message your family back in Deadwood?"

The soft smile faltered, and she didn't try to recover it. "No. I'll message them when I'm ready."

His hand clenched at his side. He didn't much like her idea, and that surprised him. Even the day before, he'd told her she didn't have to contact her family, but when she posed it, just that way, it felt like keeping their wedding a secret. But then, her brother-in-law, who'd acted as her father, was quite set in his ways. She probably agreed that Beau wouldn't give his blessing to the union. Then Daisy would feel obligated to obey the man and walk away.

"Join me for lunch?" He opened the gate for her.

"I need to put away my machine, first. I risk someone tampering with it if I don't. We can't have anyone marring the court records."

He didn't have a chance to answer, she turned from him and was gone in a flash, back to her little desk, collecting everything and heading out the back door. A few minutes later, she returned, with a hat and thin cotton gloves on, ready to go.

When Daisy was his wife, she wouldn't have to work anymore. She could keep his home and live a life she'd never been afforded as the daughter of a rancher's foreman. She'd worked hard, but never again. It was one of the main reasons he'd never fought when his parents had insisted he go to law school. His profession was just another thing he'd done to make himself more of a draw to Daisy.

LUNCH WITH ELIAS had been quiet, almost too quiet, like

he was afraid to broach something with her. She'd been angry with him the evening before but didn't want to bring up why. It wasn't her place to say that she desired romantic love. Especially not at a lunch table.

Daisy returned to work, but she'd been able to turn her thoughts to little else the rest of the day. Elias sat in the back of the courtroom, watching her intently. Since she still had to work, she was unable to turn to him, nor check if he was watching her or the court, but her skin prickled as if he might be watching her. When the bailiff finally announced the closing of session, she was more than ready to be finished. Yet, she still had to go back to her little office and type up the many hours of cases she'd done that day.

When the court emptied, save for her and Elias, she was just as nervous as she'd been all those years ago under the maple tree, waiting for him to talk to her. He wore a smart pinstriped suit and tie, the most handsome man in the room. Daisy took her focus off of him for a moment as she rolled up the long sheet of paper and waited for him to come forward, so they could talk. He took his time getting to her, as if he were just as nervous as she was. He couldn't be, though, a lawyer would be used to speaking in court, making his point, his wits always about him. He had no reason to be nervous about talking to her.

"I know you've had a long day, but would you like to come and see my home before supper?" He had a hopeful slant to his brow, and though she didn't want to, she had to refuse.

Beau, who had been a father to her for most of her life, would already be hurt that she hadn't come to him before getting married. If she went to a man's home, no matter how respected the man was, she would be putting herself and her reputation in danger.

"I'm sorry, Elias. I'm not finished with my day. I've got at least a few hours of typing yet to do. I will be so tired when I'm done. I'll probably go home, eat by myself, and retire, so I'll be fresh and ready for tomorrow." She prayed he would understand her desire to be ready for him. It wasn't every day a woman got married, and she was still uncertain of what her wedding day would entail. He'd hinted they would do little more than dwell together, but that didn't seem like much of a marriage at all. To her sisters, the living together portion was not the part that kept them from loneliness. A marriage was built on so many things, the least of which was shared space.

Elias frowned and clasped his hands together, his disappointment evident in the furrows on each side of his strong lips. "Will you be expected to work such long hours all the time?"

His disapproval took her aback. She worked hard, and the judge approved of her work and how clean her files were.

"I work the hours I need to and do them as quickly as possible. I don't want to do a poor job."

"I didn't think you would, but once you're my wife, will you still work so many hours? You'll have a home to look after."

The back of her neck bristled as anger scuttled around inside her. Unless he lived in a mansion, she should have no trouble caring for his home. It couldn't be all that different from her own apartment. "I don't think your house will need any more care with me in it than it did with only you. Since I work the same hours you do, the house shouldn't need any more attention."

He took a step back and his eyes widened slightly. Daisy bit her lip. She'd offended him, the man who'd crossed most of a country to come marry her. Lonely, old Daisy Arnsby, the quiet court reporter. First, she'd showed him nothing but anger she couldn't explain the night before; now, she'd offended him. He'd never show up for their wedding if she didn't make amends.

"I'm sorry, Elias. I didn't mean to overstep."

He shook his head for a moment, but his face didn't soften as she'd hoped. "I'm still not used to you speaking your mind. You never did that in school, but I should've known you would change after so many years. It's good to hear you voice your opinion outside of politics."

She hadn't managed to quell the sting of her words. "I'm really not outspoken." Her stomach was, even now, nervous over his reaction to her, and she did her best to keep all her emotions in balance, and her face relaxed and soft. "I just feel a little more comfortable with you than I do with most people. I've known you so long, longer than anyone who isn't family."

Even with the years of absence, he was just like he'd

been before, shy and reserved, and that was unexpected. He reminded her of the pictures of bears that she saw in books and magazines; tall, broad, and strong, but for the most part gentle and inquisitive. There was no way to look at Elias and see him as weak. His strength, intelligence, and caring had always attracted her to him.

"I'm glad you feel you can speak your mind to me, but I still don't like the amount of time you'll be at work. I may talk to the judge about it." He held his hat in his hands in front of himself, as if he was trying to both hide from her and step into his new role as her husband.

Was this his idea of caring for her, changing everything she'd worked so hard to build? Even her own father hadn't done that.

"I'd rather you not. I like my job and there are no other reporters for such a small court. If you complain, he could replace me. I had to search for quite a while to find this job, and I like it."

He gripped the brim of his hat a little tighter. "But you won't need to work once we're married. I can provide for you." His shoulders stiffened and hers matched. Would he take offense when she told him she didn't want him for his money? It mattered not a whit to her, it had to be said. Her job was too important to throw in the rubbish pile.

"I had to train for this job. Many women are working now, though not so many once they marry. I see no reason to give this up." Especially since it wouldn't be a real marriage, so she would never have to worry about leaving her job to raise children as her sister Lula had. Her heart pinched at the injustice.

"Daisy? Are you all right? You just went pale." Elias took a step toward her and gently laid a large comforting hand on her arm over the gate that still separated them.

She couldn't tell him that his offer made her feel more empty inside, than full. He was offering for a good reason, she should be happy. No one else had claimed her heart and made her both a wife *and* mother. But what he offered was little more than a wife on paper. Cold. Her sister Hattie was childless, just a wife, and was gloriously happy with her Hugh, but they also shared a love that couldn't be quenched. Being just a wife *could* make her happy, *if* Elias loved her like that. But he didn't, and if he never let her in, he never would.

"I'm fine. I just need to get back to my little office and get my work done. I'll see you in the morning." She quickly collected her machine and papers and left, preventing him from saying more about her work.

A few hours later, she sat with Patches and her leftover beans from the night before and prayed. *Lord, I didn't pray before I signed that paper so long ago, but an agreement is a promise, and I know what you say about promises, even ones made in haste. I'm bound to do this. Please, help me to be happy. Help Elias to grow to love me. I already know I could really love him, beyond a schoolgirl infatuation, if given the time. Help him to open his heart, to be my husband in truth. If we are to be together always, let us be one. Amen.*

The bonds of marriage were sacred to the Lord, not

something to be taken lightly. She shouldn't have made such a hasty agreement as a girl. But now that she had, and he'd come to fulfill it, she would make good on her promise and would make the most of it. Even if it meant praying for her husband every day. Wasn't that what a wife was called to do anyway?

CHAPTER 6

I n an hour, she would sign a document that would bind her to Elias *for life*. Her sisters might think she'd taken leave of her good sense, but Daisy couldn't quite see it that way. Agreeing to go through with this was the closest she'd ever come to Elias, the man she'd been longing for.

Through the years of her sisters speaking for her, telling her just what she should do, and feel, and think, it had been natural to accept her boss's direction when he'd said to study court reporting. Her own desire hadn't mattered. Her own voice had remained silent. Signing her name to the contract Elias had drawn up so long ago was the only stand she'd taken on her own in her whole life and nothing, not even Elias's own ideas about their relationship, would hold her back. She could convince him otherwise, in time.

She took extra effort with her hair and put in a pretty

comb, more than she would normally do, but her shaking fingers made the task difficult. Would she come back to her home for anything more than to pick up Patches and the clothes she'd packed into a trunk? Or would they slowly move what little was hers as they got to know each other better? Would she even live with him right away? Answers would have to wait until lunch at the very least, as there would be no time between their wedding and when she would have to get back to her job. Hopefully, she'd be able to think once she'd gone through with it.

The walk to the courthouse took longer than usual and she felt rushed to put away her hat and gloves before dashing to Judge Cornwall's chambers. Elias already waited outside, his brown eyes a little wider than usual as he sopped at the sheen of nervous perspiration over his brow. His dark brown hair, though a little long, was combed and oiled neatly, his suit pressed and tidy.

"I was worried you might've changed your mind." He took her hand. "You haven't, have you?" His palms were cool and damp as they held hers.

She had to alleviate his worry. The way his voice raised ever so slightly in question made her heart skip. No, she hadn't changed her mind, and she wouldn't.

"No. I made a promise to you and to myself, and I intend to keep it."

Elias breathed a sigh as he offered his arm and opened the door. Every heartbeat seemed stronger than the last, and her knees went weak.

"Mr. Laury, Miss Arnsby." Cornwall nodded to each in

turn. "I assume you realize the importance of this decision, as you are both capable people?"

Daisy bit her lip. The Lord always seemed to use the most unexpected people to speak to her. This was the biggest decision of her life, there would be no going back. She glanced at Elias who seemed to have gone pale, his short beard dark against his face. Her words had not been a comfort to him, or was he concerned about something else?

"Yes," she hesitantly answered for them both.

"Daisy, wait." Elias took her hand and spun her around, leading her back out into the hall.

Her heart skittered, then stopped for a moment. Would he back out, as she'd feared? Was the idea of marrying her so awful? Her little room with her cat had seemed perfect until there had been the option of more.

Elias stared into her eyes, pleading for forgiveness that she couldn't understand. "I can't do this, not without telling you the truth. What the judge said… I felt so guilty. I tricked you. You don't have to marry me. That contract, all those years ago, it would never hold up. You aren't bound in any way. You can walk away, Daisy. I won't hold you to this."

How his honesty made her ache to relieve his discomfort. She touched his arm gently until she felt him relax slightly, but his nerves would not completely free him. His arm was hard beneath her fingers, coiled with tension.

"Elias, I know. I've known for many years, but no

matter what the contract itself says, I made a promise to you. I'm ready to marry you."

He took a step forward and reached for her waist. She held her breath, praying for the contact she'd craved from him for so long. He slid closer to her and stared down into her eyes. How she wanted to know what a kiss from him would be like. Every strong hero she'd imagined over the years, and in the love stories she'd read, had looked a little like Elias. She tilted her head up and stared back into his warm brown eyes. At the last moment, he caught himself and gave her an unsure smile, the first she'd seen, as he backed away.

"Thank you, Daisy. You'll never know what you've given me today."

She didn't understand, she'd yet to give him anything that she didn't want to receive in return. In fact, her gift could be seen as quite selfish, since she wanted his love, but had nothing to offer him in return since he didn't really want her. At least the act of signing the marriage contract would make her the only person who could ever *receive* his love, and the only person who could give it. The thought was both heady and weighty.

She would have to use all her wits to convince him that she was worthy of him. There was no way to know just what would happen if he never did. He seemed truly content with the idea that they would be fine as long as they weren't lonely, but that wasn't enough for her. She couldn't make the man adventuresome, nor could she make his heart beat just for her, but she could do her best to draw their friendship into something more fitting for a married couple. Maybe, eventually, she could even convince him to open his heart to her a little.

Daisy offered him a smile. "We'd best get back inside, or there won't be time."

DAISY'S bright blue eyes were so honest and pure, and trained right on him. Elias offered her his arm for the second time as they walked back into the judge's chambers. He'd felt the weight of his lie pressing on him as they had entered the first time, but it was gone now. His Daisy was signing the marriage contract, not because he'd coerced her, but because she wanted to. His grandmother's curse over him wouldn't be wholly true after that day. Elias Laury wouldn't be alone. Daisy might not love him, may never love him, and probably shouldn't, but she *did* like and respect him enough to tie herself to him for the rest of her life. That was more exciting than riding the roller coaster at Sea Lion Park on Coney Island.

If he could focus on the judge, he would stop thinking about Daisy's beautiful blonde hair, pulled back into a neat bun and gilded with a pearled comb. He wouldn't think about how the emerald color in her shirt brightened her lavender-blue eyes. He'd stop thinking about how dainty her hand was wrapped around his arm, and the fact that she seemed far too tiny to be with him. Because none of those thoughts would serve his purpose to keep his beautiful wife at arm's length.

The judge cleared his throat, pulling Elias from his thoughts.

"I assume you've had your chance to discuss this for the last time? Shall we begin?" He slid a single sheet to the edge of his desk.

This time, Elias had no intention of letting Daisy speak for him. He'd be her husband, lead her, guide her.

"Yes, we're ready." His very soul seemed to wake.

"Good. You know the basic parts of the ceremony. The important part of it is, of course, this legal contract. We are doing this without witnesses, since I'm here as a representative of the law. Let's proceed. Elias, do you take Daisy to be your lawfully wedded wife?"

The words were so much colder than a church ceremony, but he hadn't thought about that as a youth with his heart set on Daisy Arnsby. Would she be disappointed in their wedding?

"I do."

The judge glanced up at him with tired eyes, so gray they were almost colorless. He sighed, his patience thinner than threadbare flannel. "No, in this instance, you say '*I will*'. This isn't a church ceremony, young man. You opted out of that."

He bit the inside of his cheek. Now the judge had pointed out two of his worst fears in one morning and was making a fool of him in front of Daisy.

"I will, sir." He glanced over to Daisy, but she didn't seem the least bit bothered.

"And do you, Daisy Arnsby, take Elias Laury as your lawfully wedded husband?" The judge's voice droned on, laced with boredom.

"I will," Daisy replied quickly.

"Good, you sign here." He pointed to the groom's signature line. "Daisy, you sign here. Then get to work." He stood and waited for them to finish signing, and he slid the paper back to his side of the desk. Judge Cornwall rummaged in his desk drawer for a moment and drew out a yellow knit baby bib and handed it to Daisy.

"Congratulations from the State of South Dakota and Custer County. We find that most people having a service this way...need one of these sooner than expected." He frowned as he glared at Daisy for a moment, then left.

Daisy stared at it, holding it in the air out in front of her, her eyes wide with shock. The judge would be in court shortly, Elias didn't have much time to help her through whatever it was that was troubling her. Daisy had to get there before the judge did. She had only minutes to spare. The whole event was so much different than how he'd envisioned it. There had been no flowers, no smiles, no real vows, and no kiss to seal the covenant. All because he'd been so sure she would never agree otherwise.

He took the bib from her shaking fingers and tucked it into his vest, then drew her hands into his and pulled them to his heart. He prayed she could feel the rhythm, even through his shirt and vest. If she only knew just how much she meant to him. So much more than their short ceremony could ever say.

"Daisy, I know that isn't what you'd hoped for, but I'm so glad you agreed to be with me. I'm going to go back home and get the house ready for you. I'll come and get you at the end of the day. You'd best hurry, or you'll be late."

His last words finally seemed to break through whatever fog had held her, and she tugged her hands from his, her pretty mouth slack with surprise.

"Oh, I can't be late!" She dashed from the room, leaving him standing in the judge's office. Someday, he'd make the last hour up to Daisy, he'd marry her in a church, properly, or at least with a minister. He'd take her on a trip as some newly married couples did, but today... She'd married him today.

The bib weighed heavily in his pocket over his heart. Daisy would know that it would never be used. Had she dreamed of having children? If she did, they could certainly look into adopting orphans. He wouldn't deny Daisy anything she asked of him. They would be the closest of friends, and he would finally have at least a taste of the relationship his grandmother had been so sure he would never have. *Too bad he's so big...* Elias almost laughed at the thought. He wasn't too big to say *I will*.

CHAPTER 7

Elias waited for Daisy to finish her day and then helped her move her steno machine back to her small office. After seeing the size of the judge's chambers earlier, he couldn't believe how tiny Daisy's workspace was. Her desk ran along the whole back of the little alcove. It was about as wide as a door laying on its side, and if she pushed back her chair too far, she'd practically be in the hallway. He couldn't imagine how hard it would be for her to concentrate on her job if she was worried about people walking behind her.

"Perhaps I could speak to Judge Cornwall and you could do your typing at home? I could buy a typewriter for you." He offered, hoping that the more she was at home, the more she would *want* to be there.

While he'd expected his words to please her, she seemed hesitant to agree.

"The files have to remain at the court. They've given

me the space they could. It's really all I need, a place to put my machines, keep my paper and ink, and fresh files. What more could I ask for?"

He held back his immediate response. If she was happy with the arrangement, why should he bother with it? But if he didn't say something, would she ever be the housewife he wanted?

"Do you plan to continue working, now that we're married?" He hoped she'd had the time to think about his offer to let her stay home and had taken it to heart. He'd worked so hard to provide for her.

"Yes, I see no reason to leave. If we have the kind of marriage that you outlined, we don't have to think about little ones, or anything."

He was sure he'd heard a slight hitch in her voice. On a day when it *wasn't* their wedding day, he would talk with her about what they could do to make them both happy. That had been his goal all along, to make sure that both he and Daisy were happy.

"Shall we stop by your house on the way home to get anything? I brought my car today, in case you had more than a bag."

She laughed and touched her hair as she ducked her head. A slight pink rose up her cheeks, the prettiest pink he'd ever seen.

"I was able to pack a few things in the last day, I also readied a box for my cat."

"I'd forgotten about that. Are you sure it wouldn't be happy outdoors?" He couldn't imagine that his house would remain quiet with both a cat and a dog in it, and he'd never even asked if Daisy liked dogs.

"I'm certain. She's never spent a night outside." Daisy swept past him and into the short hall. He wouldn't argue about the cat for now. Not tonight. It was too important that they start out on the right foot. If he had to ask her to do something with the cat, they would deal with it when he'd had time to get used to Daisy being in his house.

He fell into step next to her in the hall as they slowly walked together down the stairs to the second-floor exit. He held her elbow loosely as they descended the long front steps of the brick building, and he wondered if his support helped her feel supported, because his steps felt faulty and wrong. He'd battled the best minds in the best courts, yet he couldn't think of the first thing to say. Daisy certainly excited all of his senses, but also left him off-balance, unsure.

Daisy waited at the bottom of the stairs, between the posts of the white picket fence that surrounded the courthouse, for him to lead the way to his car. It wasn't overly fancy, a Buick Model 10, but a nicer ride than a buggy. It was a bright clean white, with brass fixtures, both a front and back seat, and a black canvas cover to keep the rain off, though it was quite open. It was just another thing he'd gotten in the hopes of providing for his bride. Would she appreciate the things he could get for her?

Elias led Daisy to his car and opened the door for her. He'd purchased a scarf for her to put over her hair and left it on the seat for her. Daisy stopped for a moment at his side, then picked it up and felt the soft fabric between her fingers.

"It's to protect your hair. The man at Fitch and Willis's said that all women who ride in cars want to keep their heads covered so it doesn't blow your hair out of place." But now he wasn't so sure. Had the man taken him for a fool? Daisy hadn't said a word.

The pale pink silk made Daisy's cheeks look even creamier as she arranged it over her head, and wrapped it around her neck, forming an almost tight hood.

"I don't have a mirror, but I must look very silly, with the way you keep staring at me." She blushed deeper, tilting her head away from him.

"No, no. You look...beautiful." Elias snapped his mouth shut. Words like that had no business in a marriage of convenience. He wouldn't guilt her into loving him.

Daisy covered her cheeks for a moment and her eyes locked onto his. She searched him for a moment, not unlike a lawyer searches for the weakness in their opponent. Would she find his weakness, and realize it was her?

He helped her into the car to break her gaze from him. It didn't matter how much he cared about her, nor how much he wanted their marriage to be everything a marriage should be. It simply couldn't be. It wasn't even worth hoping for, because he could never intentionally hurt Daisy.

She sat in the seat and he closed the door, then came around to the driver's side. He switched the spark and gas lever, took out his oil can and squirted it over the valve springs, then braced himself and turned the crank two good turns, flicked the battery switch, then turned it another two cranks, satisfied when the engine sputtered to life. As he climbed in, he pushed a few levers, then glanced over at her, clutching the wheel to keep from taking her hand, the vibration of the engine hid the quaking of his own.

"Are you ready? Have you ever ridden in a car before?" He selfishly hoped she hadn't, but cars had been around for a number of years, and it was possible she had.

"My brother-in-law, Barton, has a car. He's given us rides before, but I've never ridden alone."

Barton...he'd never heard that name before. Which of the Arnsby sisters was married to him? There were plenty of sisters to choose from.

"And Barton is married to?"

"My sister that you've never met, because she didn't go to school in Deadwood. Lula went to the Spearfish Normal School to be a teacher."

He'd heard Daisy talk about Lula, with a twinge of jealousy that she'd gotten to go away to school. She'd gotten to leave the little house in Deadwood, and Daisy had been the only one left home to help with the work and raising her nephew, Joseph. He'd tried his best to soothe her at the time, and since Daisy hadn't gone away to study to become a teacher, perhaps it had worked.

"And did Lula ever become a teacher, before she married this Barton?"

Daisy laughed, and he almost stopped the car right in the street, so he could enjoy it.

"No. She was married the very day of her graduation. She was offered a student teaching position in Belle Fourche, where they live now, but she only worked there a year and a half. I don't see her much anymore. She and Barton have five children and live on a huge ranch that he shares with his three brothers."

"I'm sorry you don't see her. I know you Arnsby girls were close."

"We were all very close until my sisters got married. I don't blame them, their husbands are wonderful, but it seems like once my sisters started lives with their husbands...they didn't need me as much anymore."

The way her voice softly cracked, even over the loud chug of the engine, fractured his heart. He wanted to assure her that she would be needed, someday, that she would know what it was like to have a friend closer than a sister. But he couldn't. He'd taken that chance from her.

Daisy pointed down the next street, where they had met at the bank. Her home was in a boarding house, just across from the bank.

"You didn't have to walk far to meet me." He laughed.

She tinged slightly pink, so pretty with the scarf. "I wasn't sure if you would come, and I could always rush right back home if you hadn't."

"I wouldn't have missed it. Do you have much in your apartment?" He prayed not, his house was small. Though, he hadn't had much time to buy furniture, he didn't want to have to try to fit hers and his in one place.

"The table with two chairs was there when I got there, so it isn't mine." She paused, "It might be easier to tell you what's mine, than what isn't. The trunk, a box with a few dishes, the food in the cupboard, and the cat are mine." She smiled as she waited for him to come around and let her out.

"And does the cat have a box to keep it from jumping out of my car and running off?"

"Yes, I have wicker carrier for her. I had to have it for when I go to visit back in Deadwood. I have to ride the train, you see."

He did. They didn't like passengers to have their pets with them on the train, he'd only gotten away with keeping Gracie at his side because he'd rented his own car. People often stared at him, so it was just easier to avoid them altogether.

Daisy led him up the staircase, bidding him to tread lightly on certain steps. When they reached her door, she stopped, glanced at him, and took a deep breath. Her hands trembled as she drew the key from her pocket.

"I've never had a man in my apartment."

"I should hope not." He laughed. "But I'm not just a man anymore. I'm your husband."

Daisy's apartment had always felt just fine for her, but

Elias's presence left her stomach quivering. She'd never been home alone with someone she wasn't related to in some way, though he was right, he was her husband, and she would need to get used to sharing private space with him. Very private space. Heat clambered up her neck and into her cheeks, her ears burned with it.

"This is all I've packed, we can come back later and get the food and dishes. There isn't room in your car." She pointed to her one trunk with all her clothing and toilette items. She'd hardly been able to drag it once she'd filled it, but she hadn't wanted him to have to go into her bedroom, so she'd shoved it out into the hallway.

Elias followed her and lifted the trunk easily, with barely a huff. Daisy chased Patches down the hall and scooped her up. The cat hissed and flailed as Daisy deposited her into the wicker basket and snapped the top shut.

"You be good. I don't want to have to think about you tonight, too," Daisy whispered.

The cat howled all the way down the stairs, and Mr. Natchez pounded on the walls and yelled for quiet as Daisy tried, without success, to make it down the stairs without noise. Elias already had the trunk in the back seat and he held the door for her to put Patches next to it. He didn't like Patches, judging by the wary slant of his eyes, but he was putting up with the cat for her. She couldn't help but appreciate that.

As soon as she had the carrier in place, Elias walked her around the car and held the door for her as she got in.

Her stomach was in knots and she couldn't enjoy the ride. They passed houses that she recognized, and she tried to remember every turn to her new home. The way they were headed, she would be closer to work, at least it wouldn't be so far to walk. When Elias stopped, it was in front of a small white salt-box home with black trim around the windows. It was an older home, but neat. The yard was tidy and trimmed.

"I don't have a place to park the car yet. There's an old barn out back that I'll convert to a garage. It'll have to be done before it gets cold. It has to stay in the street for now."

Elias opened her door as she took the silk scarf off and put it in the compartment for it in the front. She followed Elias to the house that would now be her home. Her nerves took over and she drank in a deep breath to keep from shaking.

He opened the door and they entered. Right as she walked in was a small living room, and off to the left was the kitchen, with one bedroom behind it, from what she could see. Elias didn't take her back there. At the top of the stairs were two bedrooms, one on each side. She would be in one of those. Elias hadn't wanted a true marriage. A piece of her heart cracked when she thought about living such a lie. He'd married her, but he didn't want her love. He hadn't even kissed her at their wedding. She stared at the small bed, so much like the one she'd left in her apartment, and she wanted to cry.

"You may pick whichever room you'd like. I wasn't sure if you would want the south room, or north..."

Elias's voice held a nervous edge and he wouldn't look at her.

She didn't want either of the rooms, she wanted to be with him. Though it would be uncomfortable at first, it was a step toward a true relationship. She wanted to build a marriage with the man she'd promised herself to, back under the maple tree.

"I'd like you to put my trunk in your room." She didn't turn to look at him, couldn't. The subject was just too intimate yet. But it needed to be said.

"Daisy… I can't do that."

She rounded on him, and the hurt in his eyes stopped her cold.

"Please, don't ask me again. I don't want to deny you anything, Daisy, but I can't let you be with me."

He waited for her to answer but the knot in her throat made it difficult. He couldn't love her. *Couldn't*. Did he have some medical condition he hadn't admitted to? Or was it merely that he didn't want to.

"Here is fine." She choked and turned her back on him. So far, being married was even lonelier than actually being alone had been. Patches had never made her feel like she wasn't worthy. She heard the scuffing of Elias's shoes as he left her to go get her trunk from the car. She would need to go rescue Patches, but first, she needed to collect herself. Tears burned behind her eyes, but she wouldn't let them fall, or at least she wouldn't let *him* know what his words had done.

Back downstairs, Daisy opened the cupboards and

found the fixings for a dinner. There was no way to know how much Elias usually ate. She'd never eaten a meal with him, so she had to guess. Elias came back in with the trunk and didn't say a word as he took it up the stairs. When he returned, he avoided her again and went back outside to retrieve Patches for her.

The cat howled as Elias closed the front door, and his dog came bounding out from his room behind the kitchen, the room she'd noticed was there, but he hadn't shown her. The dog was welcome in his room, but his wife was not. The tears she'd fought returned, and she stirred the simple dinner of ham and eggs vigorously to keep from sobbing.

What was so wrong with her? Was she really so horrible in looks or deportment that he couldn't even stand to lay next to her? Her sister, Ruby, who had acted as her mother for most of her life, had said that sleeping next to her husband was one of the most precious things about being married. Knowing that he was there, next to her, helped her sleep better than ever before, and now she couldn't sleep without him there. It was just another loss to add to her growing list on a day where happiness should've reigned.

Elias stood behind her and scanned over her shoulder. "That smells wonderful. Thank you."

Daisy bit her tongue to keep in the scathing remark that had flown to her mouth. She took a deep breath.

"I'm your wife. Isn't this part of why you married me?" She grabbed a kitchen towel and moved the pan to the back burner. She slid out from between him and the stove.

Just being near him made her skin tingle as if it wanted to be touched. But there would be none of that. She opened two cupboards before finding the plates. She'd made it to the table before she realized Elias hadn't answered her question yet. When she glanced up at him, he had his arms crossed over his chest and he was staring at her. His buttery chocolate eyes searched hers.

"I hope you don't think I married you only to be my housekeeper. If that were the case, I could've just hired someone."

This time her voice would not be quelled. "And just why didn't you? You don't want me here, Elias. You refused to look for anyone else, and you wouldn't walk away, even when I released you of your obligation. Yet your every word says you don't want me here. I need to know, why are we married, Elias?"

CHAPTER 8

The whole evening kept playing in Elias's head and, for the life of him, he couldn't figure out where he'd gone wrong. Everything seemed fine while they were at Daisy's apartment, then they'd come home, and he'd shown her his house. She'd offered to be with him, a most valiant offer, but he couldn't make her do such a thing. Now, he couldn't shake the idea that she wasn't satisfied with his house, or him. Had she assumed the house would be bigger, since he was a lawyer?

Then she'd asked him why he'd married her at all, and he hadn't been able to answer. How could he say that he'd loved her even back in school, that he couldn't stand even the idea of her with anyone else? He couldn't tell her that he selfishly wanted her with him, and that in his need, he'd denied her a real marriage. She would hate him. If he hadn't shoved his way back into her life, she would've found someone to love her and who she could love in return. She could've found another man, was too beautiful and intelligent not to, but for him, there was no one else. The guilt of his duplicity ate away at him and he'd been unable to do little more than stare at her all evening. Her question hung between them. *Why?*

After they'd eaten, he moved to his chair in the living room with Gracie, and Daisy had cleaned up, then went up the stairs to bed without a word to him. The night was so unresolved, and morning wouldn't be any better. So, he had to come up with an answer for her, some words to make her feel like she belonged with him. It should've been easy, he was a lawyer, yet he'd found his talent mighty lacking lately. Finding the loophole in any situation was his specialty. But how long could he keep up a lie? At some point, he would have to admit to her that he loved her, even though he couldn't act on that love. It might even ruin the friendship they had. What if the issue between them wasn't the question, but truly was his home? He could do nothing about that.

After a night of thinking, the morning held no answers. Elias shoved out of bed and glanced at the empty side. If only he *weren't* the man the Lord created him to be, then he might appeal to Daisy. If only he'd been born to another family where men weren't so tall. If she found him attractive, they could've shared everything a married couple did, and he wouldn't have to be tempted every time he looked at her. A man had no business making his wife a temptation, a wife was supposed to keep him from the temptation of lust.

On the other end of the short hall, the soft sounds of someone moving around his house filled his ears. Daisy was already awake. It wasn't even light yet. Though he spent his life facing situations most people wouldn't want to face, this morning, he would've gladly let someone else handle the task. Daisy was too quiet to ever confront him about her question, yet it obviously hurt her, and they wouldn't be able to move on without taking the problem in hand.

Elias dressed quickly and walked to his shaving stand where he splashed cool water on his face. He could spend time trimming his beard, but it would just draw out the inevitable. A problem like the one that hung between them from the night before needed to be faced, not avoided, or it would grow.

As he came out of his room, Daisy's soft humming stopped, and the soft thumping of Gracie's tail began. Elias stopped at the entrance to the kitchen. Daisy turned from him and scooped a pile of eggs onto a plate. She kept her back to him as she turned and slid the full plate to the spot where he'd sat the night before. Gracie didn't move from under the table, so Daisy must have let her outside already that morning. He'd been awake yet hadn't heard.

He waited for Daisy to sit, but she washed the pan and set it to dry on the counter and then went back up the stairs, leaving him alone to eat his breakfast. He said a quick prayer before even looking at his eggs, then sighed as he stared down at them. They were perfect, fluffy, bright yellow scrambled eggs. Just the way he liked them. He couldn't even remember how Daisy would've known that he preferred them that way.

"Did she say anything to you, girl?" He stared down at his liver and white dog, with giant brown eyes.

Gracie laid her head on Elias's knee and glanced at him for a few seconds, then shifted her gaze away.

"How was your first night with the cat? I didn't hear any trouble."

Elias didn't really expect the dog to answer, but the house was too full to be so quiet, and he couldn't stand it. Daisy was here. He wasn't supposed to feel so alone anymore. Yet, here he was, talking to his dog when the woman he loved was just up the stairs, ignoring him.

The kitchen was tidy, neat as a pin, and much cleaner than when he'd left it the night before. He couldn't just leave his dirty plate for her to wash, not when she already felt like an unpaid housekeeper. He washed his own plate and tossed out the wash water for her.

There wasn't a peep from up the stairs and finally, he went back to his room to trim and shave and finish preparing for his day. Just as he'd lathered his face for his shave, the front door opened and closed quietly. Daisy had left for the day without speaking a word to him. His chest filled with lead. He'd been mocked and disdained for his size for the entirety of his life, but Daisy's silence hit the hardest.

To MAKE it to work on time, Daisy left the house a full hour before her scheduled start time. She'd been awake for hours, anyway. Elias hadn't been able to answer a simple question. Why had he married her? There were many possible answers that were pleasant enough, but to come up with nothing...not even the same old answer he'd always given that they wouldn't be alone...was revealing and painful. She couldn't face him.

He didn't want to kiss her, or hold her, he didn't want to be near her, but he needed and wanted her to stay at home. There was nothing else she could possibly believe except that he wanted her to cook and clean for him, to look after his dog and keep her cat out of the way. She'd have to find time to do his shopping and his laundry, all for the honor of sleeping under his roof, but never *with him* as a wife should. It made tears well up behind her eyes. While she'd always known she was plain, it had never been so abundantly and blatantly clear as the morning after her wedding night.

She wasn't a wife, not really. She'd signed her name, but had never said her vows before God, there hadn't even *really* been vows. The tears that had threatened a moment before released.

"What have I done?" She swiped them away, though no one would see. Beau and Ruby had always told her that she had the choice to marry whomever she wanted, they wouldn't stand in her way if she'd found love. It was one of the biggest decisions she would ever make, one not to be taken lightly. Her father, the one she could barely remember, had threatened to arrange all of their marriages. She'd done just that. Now, she wished Beau and Ruby had taken more time to guide her. They may have talked some sense into her. It was too late now; the papers were signed. She was a married woman.

Daisy looked down at her plain narrow skirt that she'd tailored to match the fashions she'd seen in the catalogs. She'd always been somewhat small compared to her sisters, and the store never carried clothes that fit her well. She was a few inches shorter and often had to stand on her toes to reach things others did not. She'd never been called pretty, though her sisters were.

Her sisters, Hattie and Eva, had golden hair, while hers was merely blond. Lula's curls were beautiful, her own hair was only a little curly, not to the fashion of tight spirals. It seemed no matter what she tried, nothing quite worked out. Not with her looks, her education, her job, and now with her spouse.

Daisy rushed up the front stairs of the courthouse, the white concrete gleaming in the morning sun. It reminded her that even cold things, like the halls of justice, could reflect light. She had to find the light, the good, in her marriage and make that better.

Since she'd reached the courthouse before her usual start, she set to typing up the unfinished files from the day before. Now, she regretted leaving early the day before. What had the night given her besides tension in her belly? She should've had a lovely wedding evening. Instead, she'd gone home with her husband to find out that no matter how nervous he was around her, it wasn't because he wanted her affection as she wanted his. She'd only managed to disrupt the quiet of his house.

He was handsome enough to find a beautiful wife, yet he'd yoked himself to her. Out of some distant loyalty that he should've forgotten the moment he left Deadwood. Hadn't she done the same? She'd made that agreement under the tree because she'd been so infatuated with Elias that she couldn't say no. Even knowing the contract was a farce, she wouldn't break it. What good was her word if she did? Yet, she'd offered him freedom from it and he'd refused.

There were no answers and he wasn't offering anything. What option did she have? She'd agreed to be a good and dutiful wife, that included doing all those things he expected of her. But what of her own needs and desires? Didn't they account for anything?

Alma Potters, a graying historian, who used to take dictation in the courthouse before Daisy, waited for her at her desk. "Daisy, I just had to come find you. Martin is missing."

Daisy pulled another chair over into her alcove and took Alma's hands in her own. She could think of someone else's problems, that would take her mind off of her own.

"When did you see him last?" Martin was Alma's husband and sometimes got it in his head that he was capable of doing things that he'd done as a much younger man, like ride unbroken horses ... through town.

"He was at home when I left yesterday morning. I

kissed him goodbye and told him I'd be home by my usual time, but he wasn't there when I returned. I usually get an idea when he's going to go on a lark, but this time he said nothing. He usually starts talking about doing things and then I'll get him settled down. Sometimes it works, sometimes not." Alma wrung her hands in her lap. "I don't even know where to begin looking. The sheriff warned me not to let him out again. If he pulls something, I'll lose my job, because they'll tell me I need to be home with him. How do we eat if I can't work? Martin can't farm anymore."

Daisy bit her lip. The man that Elias was representing, who'd been taken into custody two days before, was Martin's cousin, and they were rarely apart. "Do you think he's gone over to the jail to visit Saunders?"

Alma shook her head. "I checked there already. The bailiff said that they haven't seen him."

It was possible they weren't telling the truth at the jail. Everyone in town looked out for Martin and assumed that Alma would be angry. The town had known about Martin's episodes for a long time before his wife was involved, and Daisy had learned, from quietly sitting in the courtroom where people gossiped, that this had been happening for years.

Daisy handed Alma a kerchief. "Let me ask around quietly today and see what I can find out. Perhaps when you get back home tonight, he'll be waiting for you." Though she doubted it. Martin never seemed to return to normal without a little help, and things had gotten much worse the older he got.

"Thank you, dear. Please, don't tell the judge. He'll either tell the sheriff and I'll be in trouble, or I'll lose my job. They've already said there may not be much of a need for me anymore." Her bony jaw trembled. "I don't know anything else."

"Don't you worry, Alma. If you can't work here, we'll see if the city would be willing to pay for you to help at the Henry Way Museum. You could work there with Martin by your side, where you can keep an eye on him."

Alma ducked her head. "Thank you, Daisy. I didn't know who else to turn to. You've always been so kind." She dabbed at her eye and sniffled loudly.

Kind. That's what she would need to be with her husband, and exactly what she *hadn't* been that morning. She had to show him kindness to win his love, not ignore him because she was in a pique she couldn't talk to him about. She had to be herself, the Daisy she was with everyone else. Her husband deserved her best, not what was left. She could never expect his love if she didn't.

"Don't worry about it a moment more. I'll be discreet, and we'll find Martin. Someone must have seen him. I'll talk to you later today and we'll see if I can figure anything out."

Alma stood and pushed Daisy's chair back under her desk, leaving her kerchief on the edge. "I'll do that. I'd best get back to work. I don't want them to find even more reasons to replace me." She tried to smile, but it quivered and faltered. Poor Alma worked so hard for the man she loved, and he never thanked her or ever realized what he put her through.

"Men can be such infernal creatures." Alma said, as she turned to leave.

"Amen." Daisy mouthed back as she pushed the other chair back into its place.

CHAPTER 9

Patches was from the Devil, Elias was certain of it. From the moment Daisy left, the cat tormented Gracie. She would hide in the smallest of places until his poor dog would walk by, then she would jump out, claws extended, and make a horrific noise, landing on Gracie's back and screeching. His stalwart companion would race in a circle to attempt to unseat the beast, and when that had been accomplished, Patches would hide yet again for the whole scene to replay.

Elias had finally locked the cat in Daisy's room and prayed she wouldn't wreck anything, but he couldn't abide another moment of the cat. That was one aspect of a wife he hadn't bargained for. Yet, he'd expected Daisy to move to his home, take his name, accept his furniture and his rules. He should put up with the thing just to even the score. The cat had seemed like a little issue, until he'd had to chase her.

The beast sat up in Daisy's room, howling as if it were dying. It wasn't, though he'd almost hoped. When he'd gone up to check on it, it had dashed out of the room between his legs and raced around the house faster than the chickens he'd had to catch when he was a boy. It was a nuisance, and now that it was safely behind the door once again, he could finally relax and work on his case.

Saunders would go before the judge the following day, for making a threat against a neighbor. The neighbor had purchased a new car and the engine was louder than Mr. Saunders wanted to hear, so he'd told him to shut it off, or he'd make sure it never ran again. He was now in jail to keep him from making good on that promise.

Problem was, a threat meant nothing, at least not until he was armed and ready to make good on it. People made threats all the time, it didn't mean they would actually do anything. His client had a right to peace and quiet as much as his neighbor had a right to his car. Therein was the problem. He'd have to think on it some more, but that would have to come after Daisy returned home and quieted down her cat. He couldn't think with all the howling.

Gracie laid under his chair, her head draped over her paws, with scratches behind her ears. She'd never asked for such treatment in her own home and it hurt his conscience to look at her, knowing it was his invitation that had earned her the wounds.

"I'm sorry, girl. I wonder if I haven't made the biggest mistake of my life. I was so sure I wanted Daisy here and thought just having her with me would make me happy. But, *she* wasn't happy last night or this morning. Being with me doesn't please her as much as it does me, and now I feel selfish for following through with it." He leaned over and gently patted the dog on her back, avoiding her ears so the scratches wouldn't hurt. The dog grunted and sprang up at the attention, resting her chin on his leg.

Gracie looked up at him with her big, brown, plaintive eyes that were shiftier than a humming bird in a flower patch.

"I know you don't like the cat, and I don't like making Daisy unhappy. Maybe I should talk to her tonight. If being here makes her unhappy, we could get an annulment. The judge would think that we'd wasted his time, but I won't force Daisy to stay here and I can't keep that cat." The offending beast let off a howl fit to wake the dead, and Elias sighed.

Someone rapped gently on his door and he tugged his pocket watch from its chain. He should've gone to pick up Daisy an hour before. If he had, it would've allowed her time after her regular day to type up all her documents. He rushed from his chair to answer the door and grabbed his driving jacket as he went to see who'd knocked. He'd have to rush to pick her up.

He swung the door open and Daisy stood on his stoop. She hadn't called him, hadn't even felt comfortable enough to walk into her new home. She was both his wife, and a stranger.

"I'm sorry. It still doesn't feel right to just walk in... I had to knock, it's not my home yet." She blushed and ducked her head as she rushed past him.

"I'm so sorry. I should've gone to pick you up, but—"

Patches took that instant to screech from the confines of Daisy's room. Daisy's eyes went wide as she rushed through the house. She yanked off her coat and tossed it on a chair as she dashed toward the stairs, leaving him at the door.

He raced after her, hoping to explain. If Daisy were mad at him, he'd beg for her forgiveness. "Nothing is wrong with her, please don't let her out. She's been tormenting Gracie all day long."

"Tormenting?" Daisy stopped for a moment mid-stride, halfway up the stairs, and she turned back to him, her eyes narrowed. "Are you telling me my poor cat has been locked in my room all day with nowhere to do her business?"

He hadn't thought of that. "I didn't know what else to do. Look at Gracie's neck." He stood back so Daisy could see from the stairs. The red gashes stood out, harsh on the against the white fur on Daisy's back.

"There has to be some other way, some compromise we can come to, that won't involve locking her up all day in my room, my poor baby." Daisy opened her door and all the caterwauling stopped immediately. Patches rubbed against the door jamb, then against Daisy's legs as she slowly exited. It was smart enough not to go anywhere near him.

"I don't see how Patches could do such a thing. She is so sweet and kind. I've never had trouble with her."

He wouldn't argue with her. He'd been there all day and she had not, but he wouldn't start an argument with the first words his wife had spoken to him all day. "You've never left her alone in a strange house with a dog before." He pointed out.

She picked up the cat, burying her face in its neck, and Elias couldn't tear his gaze from her. Daisy closed her eyes and smiled as she brushed her cheek over the cat's head, and Patches purred. Daisy would never be that close to him, that happy with him, that comfortable with him. No one would. He wasn't able to ever make her happy. It was best that he let her go.

Daisy glanced at him and flushed pink, letting the cat jump from her hands. She crossed her arms over her chest and put on a defensive mask of indifference. The one he was used to seeing from all other women.

"I'll go downstairs and start supper. I may be home a little late tomorrow, if I need to do the shopping. Do you have an account anywhere or should I just take cash and a list?"

She was so cold, so matter of fact. Was this what marriage was like? He hadn't thought it would be.

"Daisy, before you make anything, let's go down and talk at the table."

She waited for him to move first, instead of trying to brush past him. Was he so terribly big and horrid that she couldn't even get by him in the stairwell? Once they'd reached the kitchen, he held out her chair and she sat.

"Daisy, I think we need to talk about yesterday, last

night, and today. I'm not so sure we, either of us, thought this through. After much deliberation today, I don't think this will work. Look at how unhappy you are, after just one day."

Her eyes snapped with fire. "Are you divorcing me... over my cat?" Her chest heaved, and she looked like she might either pummel him or scream. He didn't much like either option.

"No, Daisy, this isn't about the cat. It's about me. I can't make you happy. I thought you would be, just being here with me. I thought we would be just as comfortable as we once were. But I can see that's not enough. There's no sense in us being married if we both want different things."

"You don't want me anymore? After being married to me for one evening, you haven't even *kissed* me yet and you want to get rid of me? Am I such a horrible wife that you would toss me out after one day?" Her lip trembled. "I've been thinking all day about how I could win you over, make you think I was attractive and worthy of being your wife, and you don't even want to try ... at all?" She stood and paced to the other end of the house, avoiding him.

Her words rained hot coal on his head. Daisy stood so far away from him, shuddering with her arms wrapped protectively about her waist. She was so small and fragile, yet, she'd been thinking about him all day, worried about *him* and what to do to make *her* more desirable. It wasn't possible. He'd never desired anyone more.

"Daisy. You couldn't be lovelier. I've wanted to kiss you

since that first time I talked to you under the oak tree when we were twelve." He couldn't tell her why he couldn't love her as her husband should, it was so obvious. She had to know. All she had to do was look at him to see he was a monster. "But I just can't."

"Can't." She repeated. "You keep saying 'can't' but you never tell me why."

All day she'd fought against the ever-present tears that sprang up when she thought about her wedding night. Since walking to work far too early, then talking to Alma and the judge, and finally the whole walk home, she'd had to blink away the tears that wouldn't stop. She'd been sure he would come and pick her up after work, so they could get a few more things from her room, but now she knew why he hadn't come. *He'd* been thinking all day, not of how to make things better, but instead that there was no reason to try. After a few hours together, he was ready to give up and send her back to her room at the boarding house. Why bother picking her up from work when she wouldn't need any more of her things at his home?

Her sisters had all fought for what they wanted, but Daisy never had. She was just too quiet, too meek, to ever fight back, and there were times it had cost her. Silence had sometimes been her worst enemy, but she had yet to learn how to speak up. Nothing she desired was hers for the taking. Elias was a handsome man, far too handsome for her. He would find a real bride in two shakes of a lamb's tail. But Daisy would be alone, with Patches, forever.

The cat took that moment to rub her ankles and twitch her tail. Elias stood in the kitchen, where she'd left him. He'd asked to talk, but by the sound of it, he'd already convinced himself to be done with her.

"If you want me to leave, give me a few minutes to pack up my trunk. I didn't unpack it. It won't take long." She turned and he somehow managed to cross the space quicker than she. He met her at the base of the stairs.

"Daisy, it isn't that I don't want you here. I do. I want nothing more than to have you as my wife. But I can't stand to see you unhappy. I..."

Words failed the lawyer. She wished she could take that as some comfort, but it was hollow. "I want to be your wife, Elias. But I refuse to be half a wife. Either I am, or I'm not. You must make up your mind." She caved in to her desire to touch him and laid her hand on his chest over his pounding heart. He sucked in a breath and stared into her eyes, an understanding passing between them. The spark was there, but would he build it, or blow it out.

"I can't give you what you ask for, Daisy. I won't hurt you. I refuse."

She let her hand drop, just as her heart shattered in her chest. "You hurt me more by your refusal. Don't you see?"

"I don't. I see a beautiful woman who doesn't deserve to

be married to Goliath." The pain in his voice rent her in two.

"You are nothing like Goliath. He was a beast, a monster, a tormentor... You are kind, generous, intelligent." She'd never seen him as anything but. How could he think such a terrible thing about himself?

"Open your eyes and look at me, Daisy." He took her hands in his and held her palms tight to his chest. "Look at me and tell me you aren't terrified."

She searched his face. He had to be jesting with her, but the deep pain in his eyes told otherwise. Terrified? What could she be frightened of? Then she searched her own heart, because her words had to be true, or he would see a lie.

"Elias, when I look at you, all I see is my friend. Now, my husband. I've never feared you. Never."

From her place on the stair, she was eye to eye with him. It was the first time he'd allowed her to touch him outside of his arm. When she had been young and wistful, she would sit under the tree and dream about Elias, and if he would kiss her someday. When he'd finally asked her, she'd thought that was finally the day, but it wasn't meant to be. So many years had passed, yet the dream had never wavered, she still wanted him to be her first kiss.

Daisy smiled, and his face contorted in confusion. She leaned forward and brushed her lips on his. They were much softer than she expected, the stubble of his beard tickled against her chin. He jumped slightly, and she pulled back before he could back up and leave her to fall forward down the stairs.

Their eyes met and his were so apprehensive, so worried.

She should've known better. Why would her kiss change his mind? He didn't want her. "I'm sorry. I'll go pack now." A tear streaked down her face.

Elias reached out and held her arm until she met his eyes. "Why?"

Now it was her turn to be confused. "Because you don't want me here."

He shook his head. "No, why did you do that?"

Heat rose up her cheeks. One of them had to admit at some point that they cared for the other. He'd said he didn't want to see her unhappy, he'd said that he wanted to kiss her, but wouldn't. It wasn't love, but it was close. "Because we're married, and you've yet to even try. While I might no longer be a temptation to you, I've wanted you to kiss me for many years." She didn't realize embarrassment could ever burn so hot.

"You ... wanted me to?" He'd yet to release her arm so she could run off to her room and escape the terrible embarrassment of her admission.

"Yes. Even in school. I was such a silly, fanciful thing. I guess, I just always hoped to be married to someone who wanted to be married to me. I never dreamed..." Her words wouldn't come. She couldn't voice that utter disappointment. He'd said it wasn't possible for her to be more desirable, but it was a lie. If she were, he would smile at her, hold her, kiss her ... be her husband.

Daisy tugged, but he wouldn't loose his hold. "You're not frightened, because you don't understand ... what goes on between a man and a woman." This time, his ears flamed red, and she almost laughed.

He didn't know that one of her sisters had been kept against her will as a prostitute, she didn't have to listen hard to know what the mechanics were between married people, and yet, she still didn't fear him.

"The Lord created two bodies to come together in marriage, Elias. I don't know what there is to fear. I know it's not my place to set boundaries in our home but, in this instance, I will. If you don't want me as your wife, then I'll pack my trunk, and you can take me right back to my apartment with my cat. But if you want me as your wife, then we share a room." Though he still held her shoulder, she crossed her arms and waited. With seven sisters, she'd had to have a little stubborn streak or risk being forgotten.

A battle waged within him and it took him a few moments to formulate an answer. He was a lawyer and he would look at every option before he said anything, even to her.

"I don't want to lose you, Daisy, but I won't..." His chest fell as he expelled a deep breath and he turned away from her. "You just don't understand."

"No. I don't. I don't understand how my husband can say that I can't possibly be more desirable in one breath and then cast me aside in the next. Explain it to me, Elias."

He whipped back to her, fire in his eyes. His arm slid around her, up her back, and cradled her neck as he pulled her in. His mouth came down over hers, silencing her. She clamped onto his vest and held tight against the swirling, dizzying, maelstrom of her heart as it sped through her whole body.

He released her, and they stared in each other's eyes for a moment. She didn't dare move or say a word. Frances had never described such a kiss in any of her books, but she wanted another, and another, forever. But somehow, she knew it would never be enough.

Daisy couldn't breathe for the raging inside her, and Elias had yet to decide. His arm was still around her, holding her from going further up the stairs.

"Please, Elias. Tell me what you want."

He slid his hand down her back and took her hand in his. "I don't want you to go. I don't know how to make us both happy, but, selfishly, I don't want you to go."

"Then let's sit down and talk about Patches and what will make us both happy, we'll compromise."

Elias's Adam's apple bobbed in his throat as he hesitantly nodded.

She'd won this round, but she sensed another battle was close at hand. After his kiss, she wouldn't be put off forever.

CHAPTER 10

Elias held his breath as he led Daisy back to the kitchen table. She'd managed to change his mind about letting her go, even though she still wasn't happy. It wasn't fear in her eyes after he'd kissed her, though. He'd wanted to test her, to show her just what it would be like with him, and she'd matched him, even bested him. There hadn't been a twinge of fear in her. In fact, she leaned into him, kissed him back. He'd fought to end it because everything in him didn't want to stop. Then he'd heard his grandmother's voice in his head. *It's too bad he's so big, women will be plum terrified...*

Daisy sat in her chair, waiting for him to say something, and the words wouldn't come, yet again. After years of negotiating with clients he couldn't think of what to say to start a compromise when he knew he would never be able to concede. A compromise would be just another lie. He loved her too much to give in.

He took a deep breath. "Let's start with Patches." The cat was neutral. He couldn't possibly think about kissing her again when they were talking about that infernal cat.

Daisy smiled and tipped her head slightly; her lips formed a perfect curve. "Patches is well-behaved while I'm here. Why don't we put her in the old stable while I'm at work, and she can come in when I get home. That way, you won't have to deal with her while I'm away."

That would work for now, but not in the winter. There weren't any other animals to keep the stable warm enough when it got cold, and in Custer, it would be chilly by October.

"Are you sure she won't dash off? I don't want to spend an evening looking for her." Because the only reason he ever would, would be to make Daisy happy. The cat could stay gone and it would make his life better.

"She may wander a bit, but she won't go far. Though … if she's out and about, you may have to deal with more cats than just Patches in a few months." Daisy's eyes danced with mirth.

She was toying with him. Mentioning children to make him think about kissing her again. He clenched his jaw as he thought of a good answer. Anything besides those lips.

"Well, we don't want *more*. Any other ideas?"

Her softly arched eyebrows raised as she thought. "We could always… No." She shook her head. "That wouldn't work."

He sighed. The woman was obviously used to court proceedings and knew how to make him want to hear her thoughts. "Why don't we discuss it, before you decide it won't work."

She smiled again, meeting his gaze with her heated blue eyes. "Well, we could turn my room into the cat's room for a while. She would cry but we would only have to do it until she and Gracie learned to get along."

"And just how are they going to learn that?" He'd chased that cat for the last time. It wouldn't be making a fool of him again, nor would it be gouging his dog.

Daisy puckered her lips in thought. Blasted woman, he already wanted to taste her lips again, and he no longer had the excuse that he couldn't because it was wrong. It wasn't anymore. They were married.

"We'll have to keep them together when one of us is home. Train them to get along. Gracie is a hunting dog. If she tires of Patches..." Daisy's eyes misted over. "She could hurt my poor cat. So, we have to show them how to get along."

"You said 'turn your room into the cat's'." He hadn't missed that part, but he was keen on knowing her plan. Would she still push to be with him?

"I've already told you. If I'm not leaving, that means I'm staying, *with you*. No more separate rooms. We are husband and wife." She smiled, a smug tilt to her pretty lips. How he wished he could focus on anything but those beautiful lips.

"Fine. I'll move your trunk and you do what you need to with that cat, but I am not training anything. The cat is yours and you can teach her to be civil."

Daisy flinched a little, but this was a compromise. She would have to work, too. She might be in his room, but he still wouldn't succumb. He'd have to keep from kissing her, touching her, even looking at her if she kept up looking so good. If he didn't, he might not be able to keep his resolve. As much as he hated it. It was his own fault. He hadn't known what he'd been missing until he'd kissed her. His attempt to show her being with him would be terrifying had backfired completely.

"You look like the cat that got the mouse, why is that?" He couldn't help but ask.

"When I got home, you were ready to send me away. Since then, I've been kissed and I'm moving into your room where I belong. I would say that's a success."

How he hated to burst her bubble. "We'll see. I'll go get your trunk, if you wanted to start supper…" He had to think of something else besides the fact that he was doing exactly what he knew he shouldn't. If she laid next to him at night, right next to him, she couldn't help but notice his height, his weight pressing the bed down. Even that worried him. What if his weight made her roll into him? He wouldn't let himself think of how pleasant it would be to have her curled up next to him, resting her head on his shoulder…

Elias stood and went up to her room. The second floor had been hardly used. He'd had no reason to go up there other than to prepare the room for her. A room that would now be used by a *cat*. She'd opened her trunk, but most everything was still packed within, just as she'd said it would be.

On top of everything, within the open trunk, was a book with worn leather binding. He opened it. It was an old Bible. The family tree on the inside was difficult to make out, but there, at the bottom of eight sisters was Daisy Arnsby. She'd written next her name, in parentheses, *Laury*, her new last name. It suited her. Daisy Laury, his wife. So beautiful, precious, and far too small to be with the likes of him. He tossed the book back where it had been and slammed the lid.

As he toted the heavy trunk back down the stairs and to his room, the smell of frying onions lingered in the kitchen, and his stomach growled. It had been a long time since he'd eaten anything that wasn't from a can.

He returned to the kitchen and moved to peer over Daisy's shoulder. She laughed and flicked a kitchen towel at him.

"Go, take your dog outside for a while and let me finish in here." Her eyes danced, and her smile about did him in. This was what he'd hoped for. Smiling, happiness, joking, all the things his parents had. But would it last in a marriage like theirs?

CHAPTER 11

Supper had gone well, and Daisy had cleaned up while Elias sat in the living room. Gracie lay under his chair and poor Patches watched him, her tail swishing with a menacing flick from the safety of a kitchen chair tucked under the table.

Though she'd wanted to move into Elias's room, her nerves weren't made of steel or even copper. He *was* a tall man who made her feel so small, and his kiss had done things to her she'd never experienced. What would it be like when he didn't stop? Would all those feelings consume her? She was already shaking.

Daisy took advantage of his distraction and followed the short hall behind the stairs to Elias's room, now her room, too. It held a faint smell of shaving soap. His bed was large, with a metal frame head and foot board. He had a tall dresser along one wall, but no curtains on his window. She would fix that if she ever found the time. He had a shaving table near the door, with a very small wash bowl on it, and his trimming scissors and razor at the ready. On the floor, at the foot of the bed, was a small, quilted blanket for the dog.

He'd moved her pillow from her bed upstairs down next to his own. That alone was more a picture of married life than what they'd experienced so far. It wasn't that marriage was all about where she slept, but he was fighting that connection, and he'd yet to *really* tell her why. He'd said she should fear him because he was so tall, and while there was some trepidation, she knew he wouldn't hurt her. For the most part, his size made her feel protected and safe, not nervous.

Daisy closed the door and opened her trunk, nervous that Elias might just walk in any moment and find her changing. She fingered the thin cotton of her sleeping gown. None of her nightgowns were pretty. Merely long-sleeved chemises that fell down to her calves instead of stopping at her knee. Her summer one had a scooped neckline. The winter one, made of flannel, had a high neckline. But both were plain white, nothing fancy. She'd not been prepared to become a wife.

She removed her gored skirt and tailored shirt, hanging them up in the small closet. After she'd removed her stays and chemise, she quickly ducked into her summer nightgown and pressed the soft fabric to her body, hoping that Elias would be pleased. Since his room had no dressing mirror, she sat by his shaving table and slowly removed all the pins from her hair and brushed it out into long waves. It still wasn't as pretty as Lula's tight curls or Ruby's bouncy red hair, but perhaps Elias would like it more than she did.

Elias pushed the door open and he and Gracie came in. The dog was quick to find her bed, circle three times, and lay down. It didn't seem to bother her in the slightest that Daisy was in the room. Elias wasn't near as at ease.

"Are you sure this is what you want? I can always move you back upstairs. It won't bother me at all." He stood on his side of the bed in the darkest corner of the room. His tall frame cast a deep shadow against the wall. He was hunched, as if he wanted her to avoid seeing him.

His words cut deep. He wouldn't mind tossing her out of his room once again. She reached for her dressing gown and held it in front of her, feeling exposed before a man who obviously didn't want to see her.

She didn't fear him, there was no need to, and she wasn't about to change her mind. Nor would he let her be the one to part them. If he wanted her gone, he would have to say so. Couldn't he understand that her trepidation was only fear of the unknown. She feared how her body would react, and his?

"I'm not leaving, Elias." She strode to the bed and pulled back the coverlet. She climbed under the covers and tossed her dressing gown to the end of the bed, then snuggled down in, turning her back to him to give him privacy to do the same.

She hadn't realized how tempting it would be to look at him. At the rasp of every button coming undone on his shirt, or his trousers falling to the floor, she'd had to force her eyes to look at the door. Her cheeks burned hot as he made his way to the dresser, almost within her line of sight, to get his own night shirt. She closed her eyes tightly and waited until she felt the bed sway and lean under his weight.

He remained far from her. She couldn't even feel his body heat. Daisy rolled onto her back and realized he hadn't climbed under the covers. He'd grabbed a blanket from the end of the bed and was now lying with his back to her, draped in one cover, the wall of the coverlet between them.

"Elias?" She bit her lip to keep her voice from wavering. He kept telling her that he wanted her to be his wife, yet when it came time to prove it, again and again he hurt her.

"Yes, Daisy." He sounded so far away with the hard length of his back to her.

"Someday, I want you to love me. I need to know how. What can I do so that you will let me love you?" If he wanted her to stay, to be his wife, then there had to be hope, something she could do to make herself desirable to him.

His voice was little more than a strained whisper. "I do love you, Daisy, and if I loved you any more, I'd go sleep in the other room to keep you safe from me."

She clenched her eyes shut tight. That wasn't what she wanted to hear. She didn't want to move him out of his room, but forcing him to sleep on a sliver of the edge of the bed because he dare not touch her wasn't love, either.

Daisy turned her back to her husband and prayed. *Lord, see my husband's hurt. See the pain he carries. He won't let me heal him. He won't let me love him. Heal him Lord, so that we can be a family in Your eyes.*

Soft snores vibrated through the bed. At least he could sleep. Daisy clutched the blanket over her head so he wouldn't hear her tears and wake up. This was now the second night that she was Mrs. Laury, and while he'd finally kissed her, and she was in his bed, she felt farther from him than she'd felt in her own room.

PRETENDING SLEEP HAD BEEN EASY. Except when he felt the shudder of her body next to him as she hid her tears from him under the blanket. He'd prayed that she would want to marry him, but he'd never dreamed that she would want to be his wife in truth. As exciting as that could be, it could never be.

His grandfather had been just as tall and broad as he was and was the reason his grandmother had made such an admonishing comment about his size in the first place. She knew from experience. It was the reason they had only had one child, Elias's father. He'd grown up knowing that his grandparent's, and his parents, slept in separate beds, and why. His father was also a very tall, hearty man. Though, he stood about four inches shorter than Elias. It didn't matter. After one child, they had separated. His own mother had almost died in childbirth. He wouldn't lose his tiny Daisy because he couldn't control his lusts. She wouldn't pay for his desires.

As her quaking subsided and she fell into a fitful sleep, he laid there, thinking about how he could love her without the desire. What had his parents and grandparents done to show their love that he could now do with Daisy? He couldn't really recall. They had just lived. They'd eaten together, talked for hours, sat on the porch, worked hand in hand. But his mother and grandmother had each bore one child and knew the consequences. Daisy needed to get to that point without ever having to go through what they did.

The best way to accomplish that might be to invite his family to visit. That would also show Daisy that he was proud of his new bride. The tension released from his shoulders. Yes, now he could really consider sleeping. Though he'd never had trouble falling asleep on his side, facing the wall, all of a sudden it was the most uncomfortable place to be. He shifted and rolled over, facing Daisy, to move back a little closer to the middle of the bed.

He'd just started to relax when Patches made a soft, almost purring noise in her throat and jumped up on his bed, curling up behind his knees. He couldn't move, or the pest dug her claws into his calf. He grumbled and moved a little closer to the center until his knees were within inches of Daisy's backside. He was far too close, but he couldn't move more or the cat would claw him. Patches stretched out farther, reaching out to him.

Daisy mumbled in her sleep and turned to face him. Her light hair fanned around her head, and her face was so relaxed in sleep. If only she could be that happy all the time. He closed his eyes, but sleep wouldn't come. Every time Daisy moved, he opened his eyes to make sure she was all right, hadn't woken up, and they weren't touching.

When the morning light shown in through the window, he finally lifted his blanket quickly off the bed, sending Patches flying toward the door. The cat landed with a huff and a flick of her orange tail. Then Elias made the mistake of looking over at his bride in the golden light of the new day.

During her fitful night of sleep, she'd stuck her leg out of the coverlet, and her nightgown had worked its way up to the middle of her thigh. His wife had lovely, shapely legs.

He needed to leave his room. Even though he had every right to desire his wife, to look on her and be pleased, he couldn't. Urges like that had to be doused. She would have to sleep back in the room he'd made for her. He pushed off the bed and Daisy sat up straight and squealed, clutching the covers up to her neck then hastily covering up that beautiful creamy leg he'd been admiring.

"As much as I hope you had a good night's sleep last night, you'll have to go back to your own room. Your cat kept me up all night." It was only half a lie. *She'd* kept him up all night, and he wouldn't be able to stay away from her if she continued.

"Patches?" Daisy blinked and rubbed her sleepy eyes. "I don't see her."

Blast, he'd destroyed the evidence. "She clawed me every time I moved. I was trying so hard to let you have your space, and the cat had other ideas."

Daisy yawned, hiding it behind her hand and then stretched. He needed to close his eyes, but they wouldn't. Mercy, her legs were not her only curves. Elias flung his legs off of his side of the bed and turned from his far too beautiful wife.

"I'm not leaving, Elias. This is where I belong. With you."

He closed his eyes and tilted his head back. How had he managed to fall for such a wonderful, but stubborn woman?

CHAPTER 12

Saturday had always been the day Daisy had done laundry and her shopping. Elias had already gone to meet with Mr. Saunders at the jail, leaving her alone to do what she needed. She'd just set up the wash water on the stove when someone knocked on the front door.

Daisy wiped her hands on her thick washing apron as she rushed to get it. She opened the door to find Alma standing on her front step.

"Oh, Daisy. I had to ask all sorts of people where to find you. Judge Cornwall said you'd gone and gotten married." The statement should've been one of excitement, but Alma was too careworn from her trouble with Martin to ever get excited about such things, giving her a continual sour expression.

"Yes, it was rather ... sudden." She should've thought of some explanation for those who would want to know, like her church. She'd never asked Elias if he attended anywhere, but her friends at church were likely to wonder about what had happened.

"I should say. I just spoke to you yesterday and you didn't mention it." Alma moved right to the kitchen without invitation and pulled out a chair. Anyone else would be indignant over Daisy's omission, but not Alma. "Now, let's get some coffee perking and we can talk. Martin never did show up last night. I need you to talk me through what might've happened, so I can go find him."

Her water for wash wouldn't boil for a long time, but she'd hoped to get more cleaning done around the house while she waited. Then again, how many friends did she have who would just stop by for coffee and a chat? Daisy rummaged for the percolator and got it set up, then pulled up a chair.

"I see I caught you on wash day. I won't dawdle here too long, but I do appreciate your help."

"It isn't a bother at all. It's good to see you out, away from the court. Have you thought about my suggestion, of helping at the museum?" If the city approved it, Alma would be perfect for the job. She'd documented so much of Custer's history anyway.

"Well..." Alma hesitated, and she wrung her hands in her lap. She'd been doing that almost every time Daisy saw her lately. "I did, but I really think I should continue working for the courthouse until they tell me they don't need me anymore. It wouldn't be right to just leave."

Fighting with Alma about her job would only make the

visit last longer, but she'd broach it again another day. "So, tell me about Martin and what he was doing the last few days before he disappeared." At least he wasn't making trouble yet, they could be thankful for that. If he did, the sheriff would know for sure, and Alma's refusal to warn him might cost her.

Alma propped her elbow on the table and rested her head in her palm. "About five days ago now, he and his cousin, Harvey, went to visit Payton."

Daisy flinched. Payton was Harvey Saunders neighbor, who had bought a new car. Saunders was either jealous of the car or was truly irritated by the noise, making threats to destroy the vehicle, right about the same time Martin was with him.

"He came home that night talking about Harvey, but that's nothing new. Those two are as thick as thieves."

And twice as cunning. Daisy bit her lip to keep from speaking.

"The next day, he was gone when I got home. He returned within an hour, before I could really set to worrying about him, and he didn't say where he was. He came back all greasy. It'll take me a week of soaking to get all the stains out of his clothes. Then the next day, he was gone."

Oily stains, perhaps like that from a car. And he'd been with Harvey, who was in jail for threats made to Payton, about his car. "I still think Saunders is the connection."

"Yes, but Martin hasn't been into the jail. Where could he be?"

Daisy stood and poured them each a cup of coffee to delay answering Alma. Martin had to be somewhere within Custer. The stage drivers knew that they shouldn't take him anywhere, and he wouldn't have had enough money for a train ticket.

"Have you checked Saunders' house?"

Alma closed her eyes and sat back in her chair. "I can't go over there. He's got that dog, and the other man that lives there won't even speak to a woman."

"But he *could* be there. Have you asked a policeman to go check on him?"

A deep flush of anger tinted Alma's cheeks. "You know I can't. If I ask the police, the sheriff would find out. I've got no one else to turn to."

Daisy slid the cup of coffee to Alma and sat back down. Hadn't she just wished for an adventure a few days before. Perhaps marriage wasn't the adventure the Lord had meant for her, and this was.

"All right. If you help me with this wash, we can get it done quickly and go look for Martin together. Elias won't be home for a long time." A twinge of guilt tightened her spine. He was her husband and might want to know what she was up to, but he'd not shown much interest in her work, other than trying to keep her from it.

Alma took a sip of her coffee and smiled. "You got a spare apron? We can get this done lickity-split."

ELIAS HAD QUESTIONED Harvey Saunders for two hours and was nowhere closer to finding a compromise he could bring to the judge. Harvey wanted the car gone and he wasn't budging. He'd even made threats to Elias, which didn't help matters.

At least he could go home to his lovely wife and relax in his chair to think more on the matter. If that didn't get him thinking of a solution, nothing would. She'd had all day to consider moving back into her room and to get used to his house. He prayed she would see reason. He couldn't take another sleepless night.

It didn't take long to walk in the warm sun from the jail back to his house. And it did wonders to clear the frustrated fog over him. As he shoved open the door, Gracie met him, wagging her tail. From the upstairs, Patches wailed. Daisy would never leave the cat up there if she was home. He scratched his dog behind her ear and stepped over her to get to the table. It was the logical place for Daisy to leave him a note.

In the kitchen, the washtub was leaned against the stove to dry and the laundry was flapping in the breeze behind the house. He could just see the edge of the clothesline from the kitchen. But where was she? There was no note that he could see, and she hadn't mentioned leaving that morning.

The percolator sat on the back of the stove with two cups next to it. Who had Daisy let into his house, and where had she gone with them? He didn't even know enough about his wife to speculate, but that didn't stop the sick pit of worry from opening up within him.

The only place that came to mind, outside of work, was Fitch and Willis's general store. She might have gone there for a book. At the park, the night before their wedding, she'd said that she still loved to read. He shoved his hat back on his head and dashed out the door. The store was on the other side of town; he'd get there quicker in the car.

It took only a few minutes to get it cranked, then he motored down the few blocks through town, avoiding the buggies and horses that still maneuvered slowly. She could also have gone to her apartment, and if he didn't find her at the store, he'd check there. When he found her, he'd make sure to impress upon her that she wasn't alone anymore. There was someone to care where she was and needed to know she was all right.

He left the car running and ran into the store. A quick check with the same clerk who had delivered his cake, and he found she hadn't been in to see them in days. That seemed to worry the merchant more than the fact that Daisy was currently missing, but Elias extracted a promise that the he would keep an eye out for her.

Now, his heart pounded as he parked near the bank and ran across the street to her boarding house. As he raced up the stairs, someone banged on the wall, yelling at him to be quiet, but he wouldn't, he was in too much of a hurry. The longer it took to find her, the more worried he became.

Which was her door? He hadn't paid enough attention

when he'd been there two days before. He'd been too concerned with getting his new wife home than truly caring about her belongings. He should've made more of an effort the night before to get more of her things, but they had argued instead. She probably missed them. That had to be where she was, collecting her things.

Elias stood at the top of the stairwell and stared down the dark hall with doors on either side and tried to remember. He was fairly certain it was the second door on the right. Nerves clenched within him. If he knocked on the wrong door, what would it matter? They might just tell him what he wanted to know... Yet, that didn't make knocking on a stranger's door any easier. He used his stature to intimidate in court, knowing it was different and frightening. That didn't help when he needed information, though.

He rapped, then waited. No one came. He knocked harder still and an old woman popped her head out of her door a little farther down.

"You missed her. She moved out a few days ago. Heard she went and got herself married to a lawyer." The woman smiled and most of her teeth were missing.

"Thank you. Good day." He tipped his hat and backed away, finally turning to leave when the old woman closed her door.

If she wasn't at the store, nor at her old home, where could she be? He drove the car toward the park where they'd had their chat. After parking in the street, he strode along the boulevard, searching for the tree where she'd first hinted she didn't like the idea of a marriage of convenience.

There, on the bench, sat the prettiest woman he'd ever seen, with gorgeous golden waves of hair, pinned so pretty, with a few tendrils down her back. Daisy. A man sat next to her, and he laughed an obnoxiously loud cackle, reaching for her hand. Elias froze, watching as she allowed the man to raise her hand to his lips and kiss her knuckles. Rage and jealousy, hot and fuming, took over as he stomped toward his bride. His size would finally come in handy this day.

Daisy's eyes grew as big as saucers and she yanked her hand from the man, sliding to the far end of the bench, but the damage was done. He hauled the man up by his coat front, off the bench and to his feet.

"What's the meaning of this?" The dandy said, as he tried to shrink back, but Elias was too angry to let go.

"That's my wife you're kissing." He dragged the man to his full height. "I think you should find someone else to share a walk with." He shoved the man away, and Elias waited as the stranger dashed off down the path.

Daisy sat with her hands in her lap, head bent down. Guilty.

She didn't even try to apologize and that tore his wounded heart even deeper. "Get in the car. We're going home."

CHAPTER 13

If Daisy didn't look at him, she'd never have to see that hurt in his eyes again. But that wasn't right. She owed him an explanation. What must he think of her, sitting out there on that bench with Mr. Payton? Letting him kiss her hand? She'd silenced the voice in her head that had warned her the whole time she was with Payton, thinking she knew what she had to do, but she should've listened, and run.

Payton had told her all about his trouble with Mr. Saunders and how Harvey and Martin had threatened him terribly. She'd only gone over to his home to see if he'd had any further trouble with Mr. Saunders or Martin Potters. He'd not seen them since the incident, nor had he tempted them further by starting his car. They had made threats to put sugar in his gas tank, which would prove disastrous to the auto.

Mr. Payton had grown quite animated the more he'd

spoken about the automobile. Then, he'd become interested in her, asking her all sorts of questions about herself. That's when she should've left. She'd been just about ready to make her excuses when Elias had come and scared him away, probably for good. Elias had been so menacing... She'd never seen the like.

She glanced over at him again, rigid in his seat as he drove them home. If she'd have found *him* sitting with another woman, she'd be furious too, but how to tell him that it was nothing, she was only looking into the disappearance of her friend's husband?

"Elias, I—"

"I don't want to hear about it." He cut her off, his voice raised to yell above the rumbling engine.

Daisy huddled back into the seat. Beau had never been curt with her, had never needed to be. Elias's sharp tone cut her deeper than if he'd slapped her.

"I looked for you at the store, at your old room, and I couldn't find you. I was terrified. You're my wife, my responsibility." His hands gripped the wheel so hard his knuckles were white. He pulled over in front of their home and turned off the car. "You left no note, nothing to tell me where you'd be, and now I see why." He didn't even look at her as he slid out of the car and slammed the door shut, leaving her behind.

"Elias, wait!" She ripped the scarf off her head and ran after him. "It isn't what you think!" He slammed the front door shut as she ran up the walk. Her body trembled. How could she have been so thoughtless? When Mr. Payton had asked to go for a walk to talk about his trouble, she'd thought it was good, they would be out in the open. Nothing hidden, so people couldn't talk.

Daisy opened the door as he strode from his room, hefting her trunk back upstairs. If she argued to stay with him, it would be a losing battle. He wasn't ready to hear her side, but hopefully he would forgive her soon and let her speak.

When he came back down the stairs, he ignored her and stomped over to the stove, grabbing a pot and a can of something from the cupboard. She'd never been particularly frightened of him until then, when his muscled arms were corded with pent-up anger. At her. She didn't fear that he would strike her, only that he was big enough to frighten a grizzly. Ruby always said, '*you never poke a bear*,' and now she knew why.

He stirred whatever was in the pot, never turning from the stove, and Daisy didn't know what to do. She finally settled on getting the clothes off the line to get her out of the house and give her something to do out of Elias's way.

She went out the front door to avoid trying to maneuver behind Elias in the small kitchen. Outside the house, Daisy took a deep breath and prayed. "Lord, I'm so sorry. This was such a misunderstanding, and I don't know how to fix it, to make his hurt go away." Daisy folded the clothes as she took them off the line and dropped them into her basket. They would need to be ironed yet that night, because she wouldn't do it on Sunday.

No other words came to her heart. Not only was Elias

angry with her, she may have ruined his case. She hadn't planned for him to find them, but he represented the man who'd threated Mr. Payton. Elias had manhandled him, after his client threatened Mr. Payton. Judge Cornwall might see it as Elias acting on Mr. Saunders behalf.

Daisy hefted the big basket of laundry back into the house. Elias sat in his chair in the sitting room, eating, not even at the table where he might have to sit with her. He'd taken half and shared the other with Gracie, who lay under Elias's chair, licking her bowl clean. Daisy hadn't eaten all day, but her own food was still at her apartment and she wouldn't take Elias's, not when he was so angry. Not when it didn't feel like her home, or that they were even married at all.

The ironing board took up much of the kitchen and acted as a wall between her and the living room where Elias sat reading. He didn't bring his bowl back in and neither did she offer to go retrieve it. Finally, he stood and set down his book, patted his leg for the dog to follow and went down the hallway to his room, avoiding her completely.

There was only one shirt left to iron, but Daisy was exhausted. Worse, she still had to heat water to wash the pan and dishes Elias had used to make his supper. Her own stomach rumbled its discontent. If she had to sleep upstairs, away from Elias anyway, would it matter if she went back to her apartment that night? She could put Patches in her box and carry her back, they could both eat and then curl up in her old bed. And she could cry where no one would ever hear her.

Daisy finished ironing the shirt and folded it neatly, leaving all of Elias's clothes in a stack on the table. He'd said she'd worried him because she hadn't left a note, so be it. On a little square of paper from a kitchen drawer, she wrote a brief note.

Gone home to eat. I'll stay there. No need to concern yourself. Daisy

She went upstairs and collected Patches, then slid out the door into the night.

ELIAS STARED up at the ceiling and, though the exhaustion of staying awake through the night before and the worry of the day was more than he could bear, he couldn't sleep. He thought he'd kept himself from holding false hope that Daisy might eventually love him, but the ache in his chest proved he'd lied to himself. He'd harbored hope even in school and, all the years between, he'd fostered it. Now that she was his wife, it had seemed like the hard part was done, but it wasn't.

She'd met with another man, just days after marrying him. In the park for all to see. His gut twisted around the beans he'd forced himself to consume for supper. She'd seemed so happy there with that man. Laughing on the bench, sharing a happy moment ... then he'd kissed her. It didn't matter that it was just her hand. That man had touched his wife, his Daisy—with his lips—

and jealousy burned hot and rabid within him.

He had to know why. Elias shoved his feet into his slippers and out into the empty kitchen. He'd been in bed stewing longer than he'd thought. He trudged up the stairs and down the hall to Daisy's room. Her door was shut, and he knocked, once again reminding him of when he'd searched for her earlier.

"Daisy? Please come out. We need to talk." He knocked again.

Even her cat was silent. He pushed open the door and the bed was empty and smooth. She hadn't lain in it at all. Her trunk still sat closed where he'd left it earlier. Unopened. The box she'd brought her infernal cat in was gone. Elias raced back down the stairs and slid to a stop when he noticed the bit of paper sitting next to his stack of folded laundry. The note was short and weakened him right to his knees. His Daisy had left in the night. Hadn't even told him she was going. Why?

She could be hurt in the street. Anyone could have seen her. It only took a few minutes to yank on his trousers and slip on a shirt. He didn't even bother with buttoning it all the way. No one would see him. The car would make too much noise in the street and there was no need to make anyone else aware of his roaming wife, so he left it home.

The front door to her building wasn't locked, which made him both glad and concerned. He would've had no way to reach her if it had been, but it also meant that anyone else could walk in the door as well ... like the short dandy man who kissed his wife. He'd never been one to let his emotions win, but his anger built in intensity until he was running up the stairs.

He knew exactly which door was hers this time and he tried to get his breathing under control as he made his way to it. He stood for a moment in the silent hallway, staring at her door. A muffled hiccup came from inside.

"He hates me, Patches, he does. He'll never listen to me. I've ruined everything."

Elias stepped closer and leaned against the door, holding his breath so he could hear her better.

"We were doing so well, getting closer. But he wouldn't even listen to me or let me explain. I've never seen him so angry."

He closed his eyes. His flight of anger had done that. Even if he was angry, he proved he really was a brute.

"Daisy? Let me in." He kept his voice low and level, to avoid waking anyone up, and praying he didn't frighten her more.

He heard her gasp and rushed footfalls to the door.

"Elias? Is that you?"

He leaned back from her door, but there was no peephole.

"Yes. Let me in." He just wanted to hold her and listen.

Daisy slowly opened the door. Though it was well past eleven, she was still in her dress from the day, her eyes were red and swollen. Patches hissed at him and ran from the room.

"May I come in?" He could've just pushed his way past her, he was her husband after all, but he'd done enough pushing that day.

She nodded but said nothing as she opened the door wider to admit him. He came in and let her close the door behind him. Her shuddering breath turned him around in a heartbeat.

"Daisy, I should've listened to you. I'm sorry." Would she come home with him, or would she stay and they remain separated? His heart and mind were at war. He wanted her home with him but couldn't ever have her as he wanted.

"What you saw, wasn't what it looked like." Her face was so pale that it made her red eyes all the brighter.

"It doesn't matter what it was, I saw what everyone saw, a man who was on a walk with a beautiful woman ... a married woman. *My* woman."

She ducked her head. "I only meant to keep our talk in public. I had to speak to him. He was the last person to have seen my friend's husband. He's missing, you see, and she came by and asked for my help—"

"Wait," he interrupted her, "the cup I found was your friend? This man was never in my house?"

Daisy shook her head. "No, I would never invite a man into your home."

"Our home." It was the only way he could think to let her know he didn't want her to leave.

Daisy didn't look up at him, but she took a deep breath, then her words flowed like a river. "It isn't my home, Elias. It never was. You love the idea of me. You love the thought of never being alone, but you also love the idea of remaining separate, closed off from me. We can be good friends, visiting with one another, and then you don't have to be angry with me, anymore." She ducked around him and left him standing by the door as she made for the short galley kitchen.

"Angry with you?" Yes, he had been, but he wasn't anymore. "Can't you see why I would be? I found my wife in the arms of another man." A slight exaggeration, but it didn't feel like one.

Daisy stepped out of the shadows and back to the doorway. She glared at him with her hands on her tiny hips.

"Are you afraid people will talk? Is that all that matters to you? *You* certainly don't want to pull me into your arms, why get so angry if someone else does?"

He took one step toward her and she stood her ground. "You think I don't want my arms around you? I as much as told you I'd wanted to kiss you from the point we met, all the way back in grade school. Why can't you just understand that I can't kiss you, I can't take you to my bed because I'll hurt you." He turned from her. The curse of his family would strike once again. He wasn't destined to be loved, just like his grandmother had said.

Daisy came around to face him and wrapped her small arms around him, resting her head against his chest. How he wanted to accept her love, but he had to push her away, for her own good. And his. He refused to return the embrace.

"Elias. We both want love. Please. Just accept it. Stop pushing me away."

He slid his fingertips along her arms to her hands and unclasped them, then stepped away from her.

"I want to love you, Daisy. But there's too much in my history. Both my mother and my grandmother almost lost their lives bearing sons. This line stops here. I refuse to lay a hand on you, and you won't change my mind."

Daisy slipped her hands free of his grasp and rested them against his chest. Her fragrance was soap and sunshine with a hint of lemon, and it filled his nostrils as she stepped closer, her eyes bright with her tears, but it wasn't sadness there anymore. It was hope.

"Hold me, Elias."

CHAPTER 14

Elias's eyes widened at her order, but he didn't pull away again. Which was good, because it had taken more gumption than she'd thought she had to say it. But that's what she wanted, it's what she'd wanted from the start. Someone *had* to be the one to say it, it might as well be her.

His warm chocolate eyes gazed down at her in wonder as he finally wrapped his strong arms around her. His hands seemed to cover her whole back as he tenderly pulled her closer, and she rested her head against his chest. The racing of his heart against her cheek brought a smile to her face. He really felt what he'd said. He did want her, but also wanted her at arm's length.

He pulled back just a little and led her into her tiny sitting room. There was only one seat, an old stuffed arm chair that she'd taken when Ruby had asked Beau to throw it out. She'd repaired a broken spring and recovered it. Now, it was hers.

Elias sat down in it and seated her across his leg. She tucked her knees, curling up on his lap as he gathered her gently in his arms. She tucked her head into his neck as he held her. There was no need to talk just yet, only to enjoy the feel of Elias, finally showing her what he felt and what she'd felt for so long. Why did he have to fight her? Why couldn't he just try?

"I said I was sorry, and I meant it." His deep voice poured over her head.

"I'm sorry too, I never meant to hurt you. I was only trying to help Alma Potter."

Elias stiffened. "Alma Potter...Martin's wife?"

She hadn't realized he would know the Potters since he was so new to town. "Yes, he's been missing for two days."

"And who was that you were with? That wasn't Martin." He was so still she couldn't even tell if he was breathing.

"That was Mr. Payton."

Elias's grip tightened around her slightly. "Mr. Payton? The one who my client threatened?" He asked it lightly, as if he truly hoped they were not one and the same and he was controlling his every word. How she hated to tell him. Hated that it was her fault that his case was now even more complicated.

"The same."

He sighed and ran his hand through her hair, the gentle touch left waves of tingles up her neck and to her head. How lovely it would be to expect this all the time from her husband.

"I'm sorry. I didn't mean to get in the middle of your case."

"Let's not talk about that right now. I need to get you home."

She shook her head just slightly, it was all she could manage, tucked under his chin. "No. I'm not going anywhere until we talk this through. I told you, if we're married, we're together. If you don't want me, we need to be apart. A loveless marriage isn't Biblical." She rested her hand over his heart and he held her tighter.

"Daisy, I told you it would be this way before we ever wed. You knew going into it that this was for convenience."

At least he hadn't shoved her away physically, only with his words. Her poor heart couldn't have taken such abuse after his anger. She didn't wish to see that ever again.

"I want more." His heart beat strong against her palm. When he sighed, her whole body moved with him.

"Why did you stay? When Payton was moving closer and went for your hand, why didn't you leave?"

Daisy bit her lip. She had wanted to talk, and she owed him that much. Hadn't she been complaining all evening that he wouldn't listen to her, well, here he was, not only listening but asking.

"I needed to ask him a few more questions, but he kept skirting away from them. He didn't really want to talk about Mr. Potters. He claimed that Potters and Saunders frightened him."

Elias huffed an almost laugh.

"I tried to direct him back to my questions three times. When you arrived, it was the third time he'd put me off, laughing about my interest in such greasy fellows. I was shocked that he would address me so, then he kissed my hand. I laughed because I was nervous and trying to think of a way to escape." She should've held him off, but it had shocked her so much after his insulting words.

Elias took her hand from where it rested on his chest and tenderly kissed her knuckles.

"I didn't like it. You're my wife. I've been called a lot of things, kicked when I was down, but I've never been so angry as I was when that man put his lips on you."

"I'm sorry, I—"

Elias shook his head and kissed her hand again, arresting her thoughts and sending shivers down her spine.

"I was angry with you for a time, but I was angrier with him. Jealousy is not something I've had to deal with before."

Daisy hid her grin from him and wrapped her arms around his chest as best she could while he sat in the chair. Elias had nothing to fear. She didn't want any other man to lay his hands or anything else on her, either.

"I've decided that I'm going to invite my parents to come and stay for a few days, so you can meet them. After you've met my mother and talked with her, it may help you understand why our marriage must be different than most. They still love each other ... but have had separate rooms since I was born. We can love each other just that way, too." He drew her away from her spot nestled against his chest to look in her eyes. "It can be done, and we can be happy. Will you try? For me?"

Her stomach slipped right down to her toes. How could she break his heart? He was counting on her, and she loved him. She couldn't hurt him twice in one day. Curling up in his arms was the closest she'd ever come to feeling cherished. Her true father certainly never had, and Beau never treated them with affection like that. She craved it and wouldn't let him shove her away again.

"I'd love to meet your parents. But don't you think you should wait until your trial is finished, so you can spend more time with them? Since we'll both be in court, your parents would be left alone quite a lot."

He again pulled her into his arms and rested his chin on her head. "Unless you would decide to stay home with them."

"I won't, unless you make me. I enjoy my job and I'm good at it. I have yet to disappoint you with dinner or keeping our home." Unless he hadn't said anything. He had to understand, she shouldn't be the only one making the concessions in their marriage. He had to give, too.

"I won't force you, but I'm asking you to think about it. I want to provide for you. It's the whole reason I listened to my parents and did as they asked, so that I could provide for you. I don't want you exhausted at the end of a day."

Daisy stilled, even holding her breath. She was no fool. He'd gone to school to provide for *her*? That meant he'd never planned to look for another wife. She tucked that away in her heart to think about later.

"I'm well provided for. I know you can take care of me." She snuggled in closer, enjoying his strong arms encasing her. Hadn't he rushed all the way across town in the middle of the night to make sure she was all right?

Elias laughed, a short humorless snort. "I can see how well I take care of you. You ran out of my house to get supper on your own and sleep in a bed that's not under my roof. Too afraid to even take advantage of what I've provided. You say that I don't frighten you, but your actions speak louder than your words."

She had been frightened, but not that he would be angry over eating a can of beans. She'd been afraid of his disappointment. All her life, she'd tried to please everyone. First her sisters, then her lawyer boss, and finally her husband. His disappointment was more terrifying than his anger, or his size.

Daisy stretched her legs and stood, holding out her hand for Elias. He glanced at her, worry lines creeping around his handsome eyes. He took her hand but stood without pulling on her. The moment he was up she wrapped her arms around his neck. He was so tall, that even when she stood on her toes he towered above her. His eyes were wary of her intentions, but she wouldn't let that stop her. If her actions spoke louder than her words, she'd show him there was no fear in her.

It only took a gentle tug to bring him down to her level and he didn't fight when she pressed her lips to his. The heady rush of temporarily being in control excited every nerve in her body, some she was completely unfamiliar with. She dragged her fingers up into his soft, thick hair and held tight as he lost the fight for control, wrapping his arms around her, lifting her off the floor and holding her tightly pressed to him.

She wouldn't let him go. This was just what she'd wanted for so long. Him. He'd been her hero, the man of her dreams, and Elias in the flesh was so much better, so exciting and soul-stirring. He kissed his way to her jaw and she arched back to let him have his way, but after a moment, he froze, his lips on her neck.

"No..." He set her slowly down on the floor, but she wouldn't let go of her hold around his neck. She wouldn't lose the battle for his heart without a fight.

"Come, Elias. Let's get some sleep." She took his hand and led him to her room.

He stared at her, so unsure of her purpose.

"Just lie down. We're both tired and need to rest, the dark circles under your eyes tell me how tired you are." And she had every intention of sleeping right next to him, tucked in his strong arms all night, if she could. She'd put herself in that spot every night until he gave in and realized she wasn't going to leave him and she wasn't afraid of him.

Elias pulled back her coverlet on her tiny bed against the wall, sat down and took off his boots. He was barely dressed for walking about with his shirt hanging open, revealing a smattering of sandy hair over the top of his chest. She couldn't stop staring at him, he was far too handsome to be hers. He slid in against the wall and lay with his arm propped under his head, watching her. Daisy turned her back to him but didn't turn off the gas lights. If he didn't want to watch her, he could close his eyes.

She untucked her bodice from her skirt and reached underneath to unclasp the busk on her stays. Being so small, she'd never had to cinch much anyway. She tossed the corset onto the chair of her dressing table. Elias's eyes were trained on her, she could feel his stare, and the hair raised on her neck as a shiver ran down her spine. She turned to him and his eyes smoldered. She climbed into her bed next to him. Since the mattress was so narrow, she lay with her back facing him, but pressed close, their knees curved together, his chest to her back. He draped his arm over her hip and she sighed, so content to finally be where she belonged.

He nuzzled behind her ear and breathed deeply, then lay a tender kiss there before his breathing evened out into a soft snore. Daisy closed her eyes, drinking in every moment, because she wasn't guaranteed to ever be there again.

CHAPTER 15

His nose tickled. Elias opened one eye and realized he was in a sea of soft blond wavy hair that smelled like a lilac bush. Daisy was still tight against him and his hand was around her tiny middle, keeping her there, where he both didn't want her, yet felt she belonged. He leaned up and her face was like an angel's, soft, reposed, happy. *Happy.* She was happy and content in his arms. He'd never dared hope that was possible.

How could he keep from her, keep that boundary that needed to stay there, if she kept breaking down his walls? She had no care for her own safety and just continued to tempt him. That kiss last night had shaken him. He'd never even tried to see other women, had never kissed anyone but Daisy, and the sensations she evoked when her lips touched his ... he wasn't prepared. Could never be prepared for what she did to him.

How did his parents remain apart if they felt the same? If they were drawn to one another, could those feelings be stemmed? They had to be. It would crush him if he hurt Daisy. Even now, he was afraid to touch her, though he wanted to. Afraid that it would sap away all his control once again. He swallowed the dry laugh that came to his throat. He'd accused Daisy of being afraid when *he* was the only one guilty of fear. Quiet Daisy was a beautiful force of nature.

His lovely bride shifted in her sleep and rolled over to face him. Her forehead rested against his chest and she snuggled in like Patches to a warm corner. He ached to hold her, to languish the day away with her right there. They didn't need to get up or eat, not really.

Her eyes opened, and she tilted her head up to him with a sweet, sleepy smile.

"Good morning."

He couldn't deny it. "Yes, it is." He gave in to the urge to touch her and traced her jaw. Her skin was like silk. She closed her eyes and let him do as he pleased, her smile languid and a sound came from her throat like a purr. Such a good wife, but he couldn't take advantage.

"We should gather what you need and then go get the car. Enough of the town will be at church that they won't see us walking home." He glanced down at his clothes. It hadn't mattered last night, but in the light of day, he certainly wasn't dressed for a Sunday walk along the boulevard.

"We could just stay here until the evening and walk

home when it's dark again." She smiled at him and slid a little closer.

He fit his hand under her jaw then back into her hair, teasing the soft strands at the nape of her neck with the tips of his fingers. "I wish we could, but my Gracie would be none-too-pleased, and you wouldn't enjoy the mess in the house."

Daisy's face went sour for a moment and he chuckled. "Not that I wanted you to think about such things this morning."

She raised onto her elbow and he thought for a moment she might lean forward and claim another kiss. His heart beat frantically as he held his breath.

"And just what did you want me to think of this morning, Elias?" She stared straight into his eyes. No fear, no bravado, just honesty and a spark of need.

"I wanted you to think about coming home with me. Staying with me. No more running. We said our apologies, let's mean them and move on."

"And can I expect you to move my trunk to your room yet again?"

He was tired of moving that heavy thing, but she was too tempting.

"Daisy, I can't..."

"You can. You were with me last night. We both survived just fine, in fact, more than fine. I rather liked it."

So did he, but how long would he be satisfied with just curling up next to her, before he needed more? She was too beautiful, too smart, and he loved her too much.

"If I lay next to you every night, I'm afraid..." He didn't want to be afraid, it wasn't a manly way to live.

"You've lived in fear of what might happen for far too long. We've known each other since we were young, and you let this fear rule you then. If you had asked me to marry you under that tree, I would've. Right then. You didn't need that paper agreement. You didn't need to make me wait. I gladly signed, hoping you would someday return. If you had kissed me under that tree, instead of *asking* if I'd ever been kissed, I would've followed you east to school and we'd have a houseful of children right now."

Her last words chilled his heart and he pushed himself up, climbing over the top of her and out of the bed. That's what he needed to remember. She could never bear a child. Not his, anyway. And she couldn't join him in his room again.

THE WARMTH of Elias's gaze touched the top of her shoulder once again as they walked back to their house. Though he couldn't stand her poor cat, he carried Patches and put up with the horrible crying coming from inside her box. She'd had to find her cat that morning, as just being around Elias put Patches on the defensive.

He'd offered his elbow, like the gentleman he was, when they'd left her apartment, but she'd taken his hand instead. Though children held hands and it wasn't often that adults did, she wanted to feel him, not just his sleeve.

He'd smiled slightly, his ears went a little red, but he hadn't let go.

They'd walked for blocks that way and were almost home when a car careened around the corner and came barreling at them, honking and making a fuss. A scream lodged somewhere in her throat, and Elias tried to shove her out of the way, but she held too tightly to his hand. The car screeched to a halt right in front of them.

She shook from head to foot as Elias wrapped his strong arm around her shoulder and set Patches down on the ground. The driver got out and came forward. Elias held her tighter and she shuddered as he spat the name, "Payton."

"I'm sorry. I didn't see you." He stammered.

"We weren't right out in the street. You had to cross over to even come near us." He protected her from Payton, shielding her with his body.

"No need to get upset. Now that I've seen you again, Miss Arnsby, er..." He glanced to the sky as if confused, but she knew better. She'd never introduced herself as Miss Arnsby to him.

"Mr. Payton, I told you yesterday. My name is *Mrs. Laury.* What do you need to tell me?"

He frowned and glanced at Elias. "Only that your Potters fellow was over at my place last night. I saw him and scared him off. They've got no business touching my auto."

He stomped back and slid behind the wheel, slamming

his door. He pulled around them and took off with a belch of smoke.

"Is it supposed to do that?" She stared after him, the thick black cloud following him for blocks.

"No. Either Martin has already done something to that car, or Payton intentionally did something to it to get my client arrested. Seems like an expensive way to get rid of someone, but it wouldn't be the first I've seen it."

He grasped her shoulders and his soft brown eyes searched hers. "Are you all right. You're still shaking."

She'd never come so close to danger and now she was sure that type of adventure could stay in Frances's books. "I'm sure I'll be fine, just surprised is all." She fixed her hat, embarrassed at her own fears.

"Thank you." He smiled at her and it was so new it made her heart flutter.

"For what?" She'd do it again every day to see that utter happiness on his face.

"For letting me protect you, for showing me you don't care for Payton. For holding onto me so tightly that I couldn't even push you to safety."

She laughed and took his hand once again. It had come so naturally to hold tight to him when she was frightened. Hadn't even thought about it in the moment.

"Isn't a wife to cleave to her husband?" She caught his gaze again and this time, he laughed, too.

"At the risk of being cleaved in two?"

"I'm pretty sure it doesn't say, 'unless an auto is racing at you'."

Elias released her hand and slid his arm around her. "Be that as it may, thank you for allowing me to be your husband. It does my heart good to know that in a moment of need, my mind knows exactly what to do to protect my wife."

His wife. The one he pulled in close as they walked. He was the one who joked with her and the one who made her heart race, even after so many years apart.

Patches scratched at the lid of the box, and Elias slid his hand from her waist and clasped her fingers again as he leaned low to pick up the cat.

"We'd better get home, before we attract too much attention." He smiled down at her and her heart did another little flip. Home, for an entire day, with Elias.

CHAPTER 16

If she ever admitted to Elias that she didn't want to go to work, he'd latch onto it and never let her forget. He already wanted her to stay at home. It wasn't just that she didn't *want* to go, but she'd rather he could stay with her, as well. They'd never had time after their wedding to even get to know each other better, and every stolen moment brought her closer to the man she loved.

He'd finished shaving and trimming his beard and had gone behind the screen he'd put up for dressing. She'd already donned a frilly bodice with a simple skirt and now used his shaving mirror to do her hair. All day Sunday, instead of resting as they were used to, they moved the remainder of her belongings from her room at the boarding house to their home and had placed everything. He'd even agreed to keep her ugly old chair.

They had worked together all day, eaten supper together, then sat together and talked for hours about nothing, and everything, just as they used to under the tree back in school. Patches had hidden at bedtime, but neither of them were disturbed by scuffling in the night as she woke with his arm protectively—or was it possessively—around her once again. Daisy breathed a sigh of relief when she found her cat curled at the end of their bed in the morning, instead of disturbing Gracie. She didn't need her cat getting in the way of what was happening between her and her husband.

Elias came from behind the curtain wall, dressed in a handsome black suit and tie. He laid his hands on her shoulders, then leaned over and softly kissed the back of her neck, sending a shiver to the tips of her fingers.

"I won't be in court today. I've got to go visit Saunders and try to get him to agree to a compromise. I'll also try to get him to tell me where Martin is. They must be working together, if Payton saw him." He straightened, focusing on the mirror, and fussed with his tie. His eyes narrowed in frustration.

She stood and swatted his fingers from the task, taking over, soon fixing his perfect four-in-hand and tightening it just so. She flattened the wide lapels of his high button, double breasted suit coat.

"There. You look too handsome for the jail house." Instead of backing away as she should, she stayed close, hoping he would take her in his arms.

"Thank you." He didn't hold her but leaned down and kissed the edge of her mouth as heat suffused her face. The more open he became with his light kisses and touches, the more she craved. He'd been right. If they continued on this path, she would want more and more of him, much more than he was willing to give.

"You know just where I'll be, though I wish it was with you. I feel like we've only just begun, and work is getting in the way today."

He laughed, his eyes finally bright. "We'll just have to put our evenings to better use."

She giggled, and he snapped his mouth shut, then sighed. "I didn't mean that how it sounded."

Daisy ran her fingers up his strong arms to his broad shoulders. If he wasn't going to hold her, she'd hold him until he learned how. "I'm your wife, Elias. I know just exactly what you meant. I look forward to our evenings together. And our nights."

His eyes widened slightly, and she took his moment of shock to stretch up on her toes and brush her lips against his. She pulled away and he reached for her. She giggled once again and dodged from his grasp, laughing as he chased her around the room.

When she was almost out of breath, she ran for the door and he slid in the doorway just ahead of her, blocking her exit. His eyes roved over her, his heart on his sleeve. She rested her hands on her hips and cocked her head.

"Well, now that you have me trapped, what will you do?"

He smiled, bigger than she'd ever seen, and with his eyes twinkling, she couldn't breathe. "You let me win," he teased.

It may have been true, but she'd never admit it to her lawyer husband, so she just smiled back. "I still lost."

His arm snaked around her waist. "In order to pass, you have to pay the toll."

"I may be in your debt for life. My job doesn't pay all that well." What would he ask of her? Her whole body was alive with excitement.

He drew her closer, his strong arm flexing around her, she tilted her head back so she wouldn't lose his gaze, so intent on her. "Your toll is that you never forget that you're mine." His mouth came down on hers, quick and insistent, driving her to feel bursts of energy through her like she'd never felt before.

She couldn't catch her breath as he pulled away. What was this feeling? As if she could run the span of the world twice over and catch the moon in a net, like she could do anything all at once, as long as whatever it was included Elias.

"You'd better get on your way to work," he mumbled in her ear, his voice raspy with emotion.

She didn't want to go. If she stayed, would he finally explore whatever it was that made her body do such strange things? She reached for him again and he wove his hands with hers instead, blocking her from holding him.

"No. I can't take much more of this play. You must go now." He turned his face from her, squeezed her fingers, then let her go.

Daisy closed her eyes as she left the room. Those feelings wouldn't leave her as she thought they would, and now she had nowhere to channel them.

She pinned her hat to her hair and took up her purse. Her heart ached for Elias and what he'd started in her, but she wouldn't give up. The day had only just begun.

SAUNDERS CLEARED his throat once again, and Elias shook his head, trying to focus on his client. His mind kept wandering to his wife, the glorious curve of her smile, and her other curves... She'd sparked a need in him he hadn't counted on.

"Seems like you've got troubles of your own today." Harvey arched an eyebrow, the dust motes catching the meager light in the common area outside his cell. "I know I'm in trouble, but have you lost all your will to fight?"

Maybe. All his reasons had seemed valid, but they were nothing more than excuses in the light of the morning. And his mind was back on Daisy again, not on his case.

"What have you given me to fight with? You won't budge. No compromise. Everything in life is a give and take, Mr. Saunders. You can't expect Mr. Payton to give up his car, just because you don't like the noise. Especially when you haven't tried any means of correcting the matter. You didn't build a fence or even try to get along with him. You didn't talk to him civilly. It's his very first car and still new to him. The novelty will abate and soon he'll only use it when necessary, especially when he finds the cost of gasoline is high."

Saunders shook his head and slammed his hands on the table between them. "Good for nothing. Loud contraptions. What's wrong with a good horse?"

Elias sighed and considered telling Saunders he didn't even own a horse and had yet to meet a good one. It might be enough to get Saunders to fire him. But then again, he needed the job, needed to provide for Daisy.

"What do know about the disappearance of Martin Potters?"

Saunders sat back in his seat and fixed him with a questioning stare. "What do you mean? His wife keeps a pretty tight rein on him. Check with her."

"He hasn't been seen since last week, except by Payton. You know where he might be?"

He snorted. "I wouldn't know. I've been in here, remember?"

Elias bit back a retort. That wouldn't help anyone. "Well, if anything comes to mind, let me know. There's only so long his wife can keep his absence from the sheriff and it could mean she loses her job."

He shrugged. "No cause for me to worry. Martin will come around again as soon as I get out. Want to bring him out of the woodwork? Get me out."

The challenge grated on his nerves. As much as he was bound to believe in his client's innocence, there was something in Harvey that wasn't right, a little off, that made him dangerous.

"The judge has no plan to set you free until he can be sure you won't damage Payton's auto. If you will swear that, they'll let you go."

"I won't swear a thing. That auto-mobile belches smoke, is louder than a train, and he runs it all the time. I paid for my property too, and I deserve peace when I'm at home."

Every man wanted peace, but it always seemed just out of grasp. "And what will you do when your next neighbor buys one, and then the next? Pretty soon, you won't see horses or buggies in the streets."

"I don't have to hear any of them right here." He thumbed behind him at the cell. "I get meals I don't have to pay for. Quiet."

If Saunders wanted to stay so badly, there was no sense in fighting for him. "If you're so pleased to be there, then stay. We'll find Martin on our own."

Saunders cackled as he stood back up, sliding his loose pants in place. "You think you will, but you won't. He don't care much if that wife of his loses her job. She's always on him to behave, it ain't her place. That's what happens when women start working, they forget what their place is."

Elias sat back and regarded his client. His own thoughts about women working looked mighty ugly when spouted from Harvey's mouth. "My wife works."

"You just wait. Wait until she starts bossing you. Wait until your supper isn't done because she's too tired from working all day and all you want to do is put up your feet and rest, but you can't."

His own work was no more strenuous than hers, probably less with all the typing she did, yet he'd expected Daisy to come home and make meals, to clean his home...

"She's never done these things. My wife is a strong and capable woman."

Harvey went back in his cell and closed the door with a loud *clack*. "You can't serve two masters. Bible says so. Either she'll love you and hate her job, or she'll love her job and resent you." He turned away and laid in his cot, covering his head with his arm.

He didn't want Daisy resenting him or hating her job, but bringing up work always made her snappish. He much preferred her treatment when they didn't talk about that topic at all.

That might be something his mother could manage. He donned his bowler and enjoyed the sunshine as he made his way to the post office. Once there, he took a slip of paper to a corner to prepare a telegram for his father.

FINALLY MARRIED. COME FOR VISIT IN CUSTER. ELIAS

Now his parents would come. After their visit, life could be just as he'd planned, but it wouldn't have the excitement that had been steadily building within him the last few days. That would be missed. Just thinking about it made him want to go home to Daisy. But she wouldn't be there. She'd be at work for hours yet, and then she'd have to cook dinner...

CHAPTER 17

Alma perched on the edge of Daisy's desk, biting her fingernail, her white shirt crisp against her dark hair.

"I'm mighty worried, Daisy. Martin hasn't been seen in almost five days. I'm going to have to take it to the sheriff, and I'll lose my job."

Daisy bit her lip and pushed her chair back to give Alma some room. Elias had asked her not to get involved in this case, his case. Threats had been made and, while Harvey was in jail, Martin was not. It wasn't safe for her. But, she hated just watching one of her few friends struggle so.

"Elias and I saw Mr. Payton on Sunday. He said Martin had been out to his place. So, at least someone has seen him. He's not hurt, just missing. I know it's difficult to not worry, but I think you just need to wait until Saunders' case goes to trial, then perhaps Martin will come home."

Alma's dark curls bobbed slightly as she nodded. "I never thought I'd miss him, but I do. You live with a body for so long, it feels unnatural to sleep without him." She blushed slightly. "I'm sorry for my forward words, but, you understand."

She was beginning to. After spending a few nights with Elias's heavy arm draped over her hip, she couldn't imagine going back to sleeping alone. The bed would be too cold, the room too quiet.

"He'll come back, Alma. Elias told me this morning that he would ask Saunders when he goes to question him."

She crossed her arms and hit Daisy with a pensive glare. "You never mentioned him. Not once. Now, I know we weren't close friends, but it seems odd that he would show up at the courthouse and you'd be married to him days later."

Daisy tapped her pencil on her desk. She had yet to come up with a good story for why her beau showed up out of the blue and why no one had ever heard of him, nor had she mentioned him.

"We knew each other when we were younger. He only recently decided to come back. As soon as we saw each other, we knew." She loved Elias's proposal under the maple tree, but others might find it silly and she would never want anyone to think less of Elias.

"That's so romantic." She sighed. "I wish Martin and I had a passion like that, and I hope your passion grows to love and doesn't burn out like some."

Daisy's wince came before she could hold it back. They definitely had the passion building, but would love come? She'd been sure she loved him before, but that had been tested when he was angry. He'd passed the test, but love still seemed like such a strong word when they hadn't known each other in so long.

"We are working on it, every day we get a little closer."

"Still. Strange that you didn't court. Marriage is a big decision, Daisy. What if you find in two months that he kisses real nice, but he leaves his drawers on the floor?"

Daisy glanced down the hall to make sure no one could hear Alma and her embarrassing diatribe. "He does no such thing."

"Not now, but you wait. You'll come home after a long day at work and all he'll want is his supper. You'll scramble to fix something fast so that he doesn't get agitated. Then, after supper, he'll go sit in his easy chair with his feet up while you clean the kitchen. Then, before you even get a moment to sit and catch up on your sewing or anything, it'll be time for bed. And I don't need to mention the work that's expected out of you there. I'm sure you've already figured that out. Then on the weekend, you get to clean up and do laundry, picking up his drawers off the floor. Marriage wasn't made to bless a woman, my dear. It was made to bless the man."

Daisy couldn't breathe. Alma had been married for almost twenty years. She would know. "Is it really that bad?" Was she wrong to encourage Elias and his feelings for her? Should she be happy he only wanted a marriage of convenience?

"You haven't been married long, you're probably at the stage where you still appreciate all his attention. Just wait. In a few weeks, you'll wish you could just get some uninterrupted sleep."

Alma pushed off from her desk. "Well, it's too late to do anything about that now. You're married. I just hope it was the right choice. You'll be worked right to the bone with your job here and all that work at home." She glanced at her hands, thin and bony. "You may get to a point where you want to quit, but by then he'll be used to you working and he won't let you."

If Alma knew the terror that her words kindled, she didn't let on. She gave Daisy a quick nod and left to go to her own desk. Daisy needed to get the files typed up, so she could get home, but she couldn't concentrate. If she continued to push Elias to explore all those feelings, all those terrible things that Alma had said might come true. He'd been right, it could ruin their marriage. Unless she quit working. But she'd tried so hard to be the best court reporter. It seemed unfair that she should have to give it up.

Her mind was a complete muddle and she packed away her typewriter for the day. She'd have to type more tomorrow, after she spoke to Elias and he moved her back into a room alone … just as he'd wanted. He had to, to save their marriage. Her heart ached to even consider it.

THERE HAD BEEN a field of wild daisies along the way home and he'd stopped to pick a bunch of them, hoping *his* Daisy wouldn't find them silly. He'd trimmed them, just as his mother had taught him, and found a pretty jar to put them in. Now, he had to wait for the afternoon to go get her from the courthouse.

He paced, excited to see her. He'd never had much trouble relaxing once he was home, but now, with Daisy, he couldn't wait to see her. Her smile made his heart sing. That morning, she'd been so much fun. He hadn't run around like a boy since school, and when she'd let him catch her...

She was winning the war. He may have laid down the battle plan, but she was winning fair and square. She didn't fear him, didn't listen to his pleading, kissed him with abandon. If his mother didn't come and convince Daisy soon, he'd be lost and there would be no going back.

His bride pushed through the door and glanced at him for a moment, fear rippling down her face before she hid it. She tucked her chin as she hung up her walking coat.

"Daisy? Did you have a good day?" He took a few steps closer but stopped when her shoulders tensed.

"A good day? Yes." Her sunken eyes said the opposite. She pressed her skirt with a nervous twitch of her hand he'd never seen before then she passed him without looking him the eye. "I'll just get supper started."

She had been so boisterous and energetic that morning, something had to have happened to her to make her so sullen.

"You don't have to make it right away, we could sit and talk for a few minutes, if you'd rather?" He hoped she did. Her stiff back and cold words made him nervous.

Daisy paused and faced him, but she never looked up, never met his eyes. Her shoulders were slumped, and it killed him to see her like that.

"I think ... that is to say ... you're right. I should return to my room. I'm sorry I pressed you so." She whipped around so quickly her skirt billowed around her legs and she leaned against the kitchen counter, her breaths measured, like she was within moments of tears.

"Daisy?" Two days ago, he would've been jumping for joy that she'd come to her senses, but now, no. He wanted Daisy with him. She was his wife and it was where she belonged. "Are you sure? You can stay with me, but I won't push you, if that's what you really want." If he did, she might finally understand the huge brute he was.

She nodded, facing the stove. "I've had time to think about everything you said and, you're right. I've got no business making more of this than we agreed on."

Elias glanced at the flowers on the table, she hadn't even noticed them. She was shoving his own words at him, yet they sounded nothing like what he remembered saying. He was getting what he wanted, what he deserved, so why did his chest feel like she'd torn him in two?

How many times had he moved that trunk now? More

than he could recall, but it felt heavier this time. He set it at the base of the stairs and went back into the kitchen. Before he moved that thing a step farther, he needed Daisy to tell him what had happened to change her mind. She stood at the table, her finger tracing one of the petals on a daisy. A tear dripped off her cheek and landed on the front of her bodice.

He strode forward and collected her in his arms. She pushed away from him at first, but he held fast and within moments she melted into sobs and clung to him. His lawyer brain wanted to ask all sorts of questions, but his heart knew they had to wait. Too many questions now would only push her further, but he did have to know one thing.

"What did I do?" he whispered gently to the top of her head.

She shuddered and held him tighter. "You were right, so terribly right, and I'm scared."

He stiffened, the old fears rearing up and telling him to push her away before he hurt her, but he couldn't. His heart was too involved now.

"I'm so sorry. I warned you that I could never… I won't hurt you. I promise." He kissed the top of her head.

"I know, I know you'd never hurt me. Why didn't I listen? I don't know how *you* knew what marriage would be like when *I* didn't. I have seven married sisters and some of them work, yet they never told me. I'm so sorry."

Elias massaged the back of her tense shoulders as he tried to understand what she was saying but none of it

151

KARI TRUMBO

made any sense at all. How could he be right, as she said, and yet not know what she was talking about?

"Daisy, I want to comfort you, to say the right thing to ease your mind, but I'm so confused."

She pulled away from him, her cheeks a dark pink. She turned away. "It doesn't matter. Thank you for moving my trunk. I'm sorry supper is so late. I'll do better in the future."

Her words were like a dash of ice water over his head. This morning, he'd kissed her and had worried that another few days of Daisy and he'd lose all his resolve. By evening, he'd lost her again. She was back to the all-business woman he'd seen at the park when he'd hurt her. Except this time, he couldn't figure out what he'd done.

"Would you rather I take you out to supper?" He offered. He hadn't taken her out since they were married, if she was overworked from the moving the day before, she might be tired.

She turned to him, her eyes flashing a sapphire blue. "Are you saying my meals aren't good enough? Why don't *you* try working all day long and then come home to make supper? And you'd best not start leaving your drawers on the floor, either."

Daisy slapped her hand over her mouth as if she was as shocked as he about what had just come out. His house had been clean when she came, and he'd never even left a sock on the floor, much less something so offensive as his drawers...

"Daisy, what is this all about?"

She turned away from him, her ears glowing red. "Nothing. No, I don't want to go out. Please, give me a little time and I'll have your supper ready."

Elias backed out of the room and went for her trunk. He'd get to the bottom of what was ailing Daisy, because a body didn't change that much in a day with no cause.

CHAPTER 18

I t was already past seven in the morning, but Daisy couldn't force herself from her bed. She'd laid there, alone, all night. Even Patches was angry with her and slept on the floor. The cat had taken to scratching the wall by the door, leaving gouges. She'd have to find time to repair that, too. Along with all the other things to clean up.

"You're making more work for me. If you don't be good, I'll let you outside and refuse to take you back in." Daisy hissed from the bed.

"Daisy?" Elias's voice came softly through the door. "Are you awake and all right?"

She held her breath for a moment and tugged the coverlet up to her chin. How she missed her husband, but she couldn't tempt him, not if they were to remain happy. "I'm fine. I'll be down shortly. I'm sorry, you must be famished." She sounded syrupy. Over-happy. Fake. She waited for him to shuffle back down the stairs, but it was silent outside her door.

"May I come in?"

She'd felt so alone all night, but that was her destiny. She'd married a man who wanted nothing to do with her and, according to Alma, was lucky for it. Passion didn't mix with a working woman. Yet, would she give up that career to kindle her love? Wasn't desire a worthy thing?

"I'm ... not dressed yet."

He opened the door and slid inside.

"Elias!" She gasped, clutching the covers higher.

He was wearing nothing more than a pair of trousers; his long, muscled torso couldn't be ignored. His stride carried him across the room and to the head of the bed in four steps. The bed creaked under his heavy weight as he sat. His brows were drawn together in worry as he held the back of his hand to her forehead.

"Are you ill? You never stay abed this late."

He was far too distracting, with his tender touch and his body far too close to her. The heat from him poured off of his skin, or maybe it was just heat rushing to her face. She had to hold back, look away. If she didn't, she might resent him, even hate him, according to Alma. But if she had to choose, the job would have to go. She couldn't stand lying in bed, wishing he were with her every night for the remainder of her days. It wasn't worth it.

"Oh, Elias." She flung the coverlet off and climbed into his arms. He drew her closer, tenderly holding her head to his rushing heart. "I can't do this. I wanted to honor your wishes. Alma said such terrible things, but I can't. I'll stop working if I must, but I can't stay away from you."

His purposely soft touch, wound up and down her arm, slowed then stopped. "They are not mutually exclusive. You can stay in my room and continue to work. I only asked you to consider it. I didn't want you to be exhausted, and I *can* take care of you. I *want* to take care of you."

Daisy buried her face deeper in his chest, his skin warm against her cheek, and the soft down of his chest tickling her. "Alma said that you would be dissatisfied with me. That you would get angry if I was tired after work, and that you would rest while I worked. And..." Oh, that last bit was so embarrassing. But she'd already mentioned it the night before and she didn't want him to start leaving a mess. Daisy took a deep breath and rushed on. "She said that you would expect me to perform my wifely duties whether I was too tired or not, and then I'd have to pick up your underthings every weekend."

A chuckle rumbled, slow at first, then built in momentum until Elias was laughing so hard he couldn't hold her close anymore.

"I don't see what is so funny. She's been married for a long time."

He took a minute to get himself under control, but his laughter was just under the surface, trying to burst free. "How long have Beau and Ruby been married? He used to pick you up from school every day, so it has to have been for quite some time."

She hadn't thought about it, but their son, Joseph, was

almost sixteen years old. They had been married in 1882, the day before her father died, then Beau had willingly taken over the job as the father of all Ruby's sisters. "Eighteen years."

"And does Beau leave a mess for Ruby?"

Alma had seemed so much older than her sister, but they had to be close in age, since they'd been married almost as long. "No, but Ruby doesn't work. She tends to their son and the house. It must be so empty now."

"Don't you see, Daisy? Just because one woman isn't happy with the way her marriage has gone, doesn't mean that you will end up the same way. You can't be the only one of your sisters who works."

Nora was a milliner in Hot Springs, and she was very happily married to her sheriff. Lula had been a teacher before she and Barton started a family. Frances wrote romance novels, even to that day, but that was mostly from home, and her husband, Clive, helped her. Eva did charity work in Lead, along with teaching art classes, and her husband had some job no one was allowed to know about. Hattie, Jennie, and Ruby all still lived out at Ferguson Ranch, tending their husbands and anything else around the ranch that needed to be done. "Yes, some of them work."

"I've never forced you to perform any wifely duties. Have your sisters ever complained about having to keep up with their husbands' demands?"

She was sure she was scalding Elias's chest with the

heat pouring off her cheeks. Husbandly duties, indeed. "They have never said so, no," she whispered, unable to speak past her embarrassment.

He drew her from him and tipped her face to look at him. The mirth had evaporated and all that remained was the melted chocolate heat of his eyes. "If your sisters are happy and well-loved, don't you think I can do the same?"

Her insides fluttered to life, sending luscious, tempting waves flowing through her. "I thought you didn't want me," she whispered.

"It's not a matter of wanting you. I've wanted you for years. You've been open about your fears with me but I'm afraid mine are not as easily relayed. I fear that if I make love to you, I will crush you. If I put a child in you, it could kill you, and I could *never* live with myself after."

IF HIS HONESTY didn't frighten her, nothing would. Daisy gazed into his eyes, her blue depths were so alive, inviting. She slid her hand up his bare chest, tempting him to the brink.

"I'm not frightened of you. I told you last night. I don't believe you would ever hurt me."

She was too trusting, his little flower. He drew her close and kissed her, wanting so much more, but forcing himself to be satisfied after a taste.

"I leave it up to you, if you want to work or not. But I

can't have you up here anymore. You've convinced me that I need you. I want you with me at night, if that helps you with your decision."

She was good at her profession, he had no doubts. But she'd asked him not to interfere with her job, and so he wouldn't. The night had been long as he'd laid there listening to Gracie snore and wishing his bride were there. It hadn't taken her long to prove to him that she could never be replaced. Just a few short days and he was hooked.

"I don't want to leave."

"Then, perhaps I could hire someone to come in for a few hours a day and manage the cat, pick up, do the laundry, and make our supper. If that would make you happy, then that is what I'll do. I would much rather spend my evening sitting with you than alone."

Her eyes widened, and a smile broke over her face, warmer than a bath on a hot summer day. "You would do that? For me?"

For her, he'd walk across the desert filled with rattlers, barefoot, if he had to. "I'll ask around for references, but I won't ask Alma."

She chuckled and tucked herself back into his chest. As much as he loved it, he had to get up and get ready. Court would convene in a half hour. As it was, they would have to drive to make it in on time. He kissed the top of her head, wishing he could indulge in more.

"Time to get up and start the day. The toasting wire is

already hot on the stove, and the butter is on the counter. That's about all we have time for. I'll drive."

She allowed him to stand, but she didn't take her eyes off of him, either. When she watched him, he had the strangest urge to flex his muscles.

"Are you going to stand there and watch me dress, husband?" She smiled as she climbed from the bed, showing off those curvy legs that he hadn't seen since that first night she'd insisted on joining him.

"No, not watching." He closed his eyes and turned to leave the room, but the vision of her with her night dress hiked to her thighs was already imprinted there.

He rushed down to his room and quickly dressed. He'd been up there longer than he'd planned and there were few minutes to spare. He'd always been an honest man, and Daisy's honest words sparked something deep within him. The way she thought was perfect for him, as if the Good Lord, knowing how he was and what he needed, had shaped her along her life to be just the woman for him. If only He'd fashioned Elias to be as perfect for her.

He finished buttoning his shirt and shrugged on his suit coat as Daisy rushed down the stairs.

"Have you eaten? I'm afraid I dawdled too long and there isn't time for me to make anything." Her sweet mouth turned down.

He took a rag to remove the toasting wires from the stove.

"I haven't, but I'll be fine until lunch. Will you join me?" He hoped the offer would take the strain from her.

"That would be nice. We can talk about hiring someone, like you mentioned."

He grabbed her coat and slid it up her arms, leading her out the door. They would be late if he didn't rush them. "Agreed."

When they pulled out onto the street, he remembered he had yet to tell her about his note to his father.

"I sent a telegram to my parents. I'm sure they'll come within the next few days. I don't see the Saunders case going to trial soon, so it would be a good time."

"If that's true, poor Alma will wonder where her husband is and will probably lose her job."

Daisy had told him about the sheriff's anger with Martin and his schemes, but it wasn't his wife's job to keep Martin out of trouble.

"Doesn't seem fair that she be taken to task for being unable to do something the sheriff can't do himself."

"I don't know if he would or if it was a bluff to keep her from coming to him when Martin turns up missing. It seems dreadfully unfair."

"Why don't you leave talking to the sheriff up to me. I won't ask you to give up on a friend, but do take what she says with a full measure of salt."

Daisy nodded and turned from him. "I'm sorry I let what she said get to me so."

"It's already forgotten. If you'd like, you should invite your family to come for a day or two. We didn't get to have a wedding party."

He'd rather not share Daisy for days and days but doing so might cool his blood. Seeing his parents for a few days certainly would. Nothing could quite remind him of his purpose more than seeing the woman he almost killed, just by being born.

CHAPTER 19

Daisy squinted at the roll of steno paper in front of her and tried to concentrate on the tiny marks, so she could finish up her typing and walk home. Elias had told her at lunch that he had finished meeting with clients and that he would meet with a woman that afternoon about the housekeeping position. She'd never dreamed it would come together so quickly, but so many people struggled to make a living in South Dakota that any job would be filled quickly. Including her own if she chose to leave.

"Ahem," Mr. Payton cleared his throat beside her desk and waited for her to turn. "Excuse me, Mrs. Laury. Might I beg a moment or two of your time?"

She didn't want to, not after he'd tried to make Elias think that she'd introduced herself to him as an unmarried woman, and almost ran them down in the street. She paused, fingers poised above the keys, hoping he understood that she was too busy for his interruption.

"Yes, Mr. Payton? I'm afraid I'm in quite a hurry. My husband will be coming to get me shortly." He would never know it was a lie, that she usually walked home to save Elias the trouble, but he'd always seemed somewhat frightened of Elias and, if that made him leave, she would happily tell him her giant of a husband was on his way.

"Mrs. Potters asked me to deliver this note to you. She said it was urgent."

She had no interest in Mr. Payton, but Alma was her only friend. Daisy turned and accepted the note.

Dear Daisy,

I've found Martin. He's hurt. Can you please come with Mr. Payton and help me?

Alma

Something about the note didn't sit right. Mr. Payton and Martin were enemies, why would Alma give *him* such a note?

"I don't understand how you came to be with Alma when she found Martin?" Daisy folded the paper and scored it with her thumbnail as she tried to figure out what she should do.

"Alma came to me this afternoon, since she'd heard that Martin was seen at my house. She asked if she could look around for him and, of course, I let her. She found him injured in one of my old sheds, hiding like the mole he is. I don't know *why* he was there, nor do I care. She asked me to deliver that note and bring you with to help her."

Daisy didn't want to do anything with him, there was a hint of danger about him. Not to mention his driving wasn't safe, and he hadn't cared that she was married when he'd turned philanderer on her in the park.

"I don't see why you can't help her get Martin to the doctor. I certainly can't. Perhaps we should wait for Elias? He would be big enough to help lift an injured man."

Mr. Payton narrowed his eyes and smiled, though it looked more like he was baring his teeth. "Mrs. Laury, I assure you, I have no idea why she requires *your* assistance, but I'm not a driving service. You can come or not, it doesn't matter to me."

Alma had never wanted to reach out to anyone for help with Martin, afraid that people would either take away her position or put her husband away in a home. Was that her fear now? Was she reaching out to the one person who would listen? She might be looking for help from Daisy because she had nowhere else to turn.

"Let me get my coat. We must be quick, though. I don't want Elias to wonder where I am."

Mr. Payton gently touched her back as he led her out of the courthouse. His touch made her shudder like finding maggots in the larder. His car waited, already running, on the street at the base of the steps. She'd never forget it after he'd almost run them down in the street. He held the passenger side open for her and she hesitated. Elias wouldn't like the fact that she was getting into his car, that anyone would see her with Payton at all.

"Dear, we don't have much time." He pushed her onto the seat and slammed the door shut, rushing around to the driver's side. He slipped in and slammed it into gear, smashing her into the back of the seat as he rushed off.

Daisy held tight to the door as he swerved down the streets and screeched around turns. He didn't even slow down enough for her to try to jump out. Horses and buggies jostled to get out of his way and cowboys cursed at him as he careened down the street.

The door wouldn't open as she fumbled with the latch, trying to get out. Her hands trembled. Alma had better need her desperately, to have put her in so much danger. Mr. Payton lived outside of town near French Creek, far enough that Mr. Saunders lot was an acre away, and the adjoining neighbor was no closer. Though it was still near enough that his loud automobile would be bothersome.

"Where is Alma? I want to get this over with and go home." She slid from the car and waited for him to come around.

Payton laughed. "Right this way." He gestured to one of his more decrepit outbuildings. He took long-legged strides to stay ahead of her as they made their way to the shed.

"Alma? Are you in there?" Daisy called, needing to hear her friend's voice. The longer she was alone with Payton, the more the hair prickled on the back of her neck. Alma didn't answer.

The door to the shed was a handle like those on a barn door. It was shaped like an O that had been flattened. He had to turn it sideways to open, then pulled the door wide.

"Why did you lock them in?" There would be no way for her to get out if she walked in to help Alma and he shut the door behind her.

"I didn't intend to. This latch locks all by itself." He stood back, giving her room to go inside.

"Alma, answer me or I won't come in. I'm here to help you."

Daisy took a step closer. "Alma?"

Payton's face flashed hot anger and he grabbed her by the arm, shoving her into the small shed. She turned to run but the door slammed in her face. He laughed as the door latch locked into place.

THE AIR around Elias vibrated with energy. The evening sun was bright in his eyes, and he tipped his head so he could see the exit to the courthouse better. He'd been waiting all day to tell Daisy that he'd found someone to work in their home, so she could continue doing the job she loved without any guilt. His foot tapped on the baseboard as he waited, pulling out his watch. She was late.

For the last week, she'd gotten home earlier than expected and he hadn't even been able to pick her up. When the hour had come for her to leave work and she hadn't arrived, he'd gone to pick her up. He turned off his auto and dashed up the steps. The light glinted off the bright white concrete, but Daisy's little alcove had no window, so she wouldn't be fooled by the light. His excitement shifted as worry brewed in the pit of his stomach. What could be keeping her?

The halls of the courthouse were silent and dim, having closed an hour before. The sounds of people usually echoed through the building, with its high ceilings. He strode down the hall toward Daisy's tiny office, but there was no light shining out, nor did he hear the clack of her typewriter.

When he reached her desk, it was a mess of papers and files. The scroll of steno paper from the case she'd been working on lay in a jumble by her typewriter and the case of her steno machine still lay open. Her walking coat and purse were gone. She never left her desk looking like that, it would be cause for her to lose her job. The concern that had been a weak wave as he'd come in the building built to a flood tide.

He tidied all her files and put everything away, so if anyone would walk by they wouldn't immediately see what she'd been working on. Daisy's friend Alma turned the corner and her eyes widened. She rushed to retreat back around the corner.

"Mrs. Potters! Wait!" He rushed toward her, his footfalls making a racket on the dull linoleum.

She waited, clinging close to the wall, her face hidden by her tucked chin.

"I know Daisy was helping you look for your husband.

Have you seen her? She isn't at her desk and I haven't seen her since lunch. She hasn't returned home."

Alma sighed heavily and leaned closer to the wall. "I didn't want to have to be the one to say anything. I'm sorry to have to tell you, because, it's *so* scandalous." Her glance flitted all over the hall, then centered on his right ear, but never on his eyes. "I saw her leave with Mr. Payton about two hours ago. He came in, talked to her for a few minutes, and then she left with him in a hurry. He had his arm around her when they left."

Payton. How that man needed a good, swift kick. He'd told Daisy to stay away from Mr. Payton, to remember that she was *his* wife. Why would she go with him, unless she wanted to be with him? Had her anger and fear been an act when Payton had almost hit them with his car?

Alma reached out, then pulled away. "If you go to confront Payton, you'll find her there. That's all I can say." The clack of her healed slippers bounced down the hall until all was silent but the thump of his heart, pounding in his ears.

His parents would be there in two days, and the wife they were supposed to meet, had already roamed to someone else. He'd asked her if she'd been courting anyone before he'd given her the notice of their marriage. She still had that notice tucked in her Bible, he'd seen it there. It had been Daisy, not him, who gave the first kiss.

Rare anger exploded within him. What could Payton offer that *he* couldn't? What could she find with him that she couldn't have with Elias? He'd give her the world if he could.

Except Payton wasn't a monster. *He* could give her more than a marriage of convenience. Hadn't she just given up on Elias the night before, leaving him to sleep alone? Telling him he was right, and she shouldn't have pressed? He should've known the problem was deeper than Alma. Daisy's sisters alone could've proved Alma's words false.

He'd been such a fool to believe her morning regrets and desires. She'd been telling him that it was over. He slammed his fist into the plaster wall, sending pain up his arm, but he didn't care. It was nothing compared to the pain in his heart. Payton had taken the only thing that had ever mattered.

The walk back to his car seemed to take years instead of a few minutes. His neck tingled, prickling to awareness. He was sure everyone stared at him. Judging him, for losing his bride so quickly. He should've known better.

CHAPTER 20

The small shed had gone from stifling to cold as the evening wind picked up, blasting down the hills. The old shed didn't even try to keep the drafts out and Daisy crouched in the corner, her coat wrapped tightly around her, huddled in as tight a ball as she could manage.

At least Payton hadn't been back to torment her. If he kept his hands off of her, someone might figure out where she was. Alma would know, *if* she'd actually written the note. If Alma told Elias, he could find her. When she didn't show up at home, he would come to look for her. It had to be past the hour she would usually arrive home. But, even if he thought to look at Mr. Payton's, he wouldn't think to look out in his sheds. It would make no sense for her to be in one.

The small building was empty except for a few tools,

and the floor was little more than some boards laid on the dirt. She would be filthy, but she'd take the filth if there was a way to break free. The shed had no windows, only the door with the barn latch on it that she couldn't turn from the inside.

"Daisy?" Alma's voice whispered from outside.

"Alma? Is that you? Get me out!" Daisy sprang to her feet and rushed to the door, banging on it so Alma would know which shed she was in.

"Daisy, hush now. I can't let you out. Payton promised that when the judge lets Saunders go, then Mr. Payton will set Martin free. I told Elias you were here, and Saunders already told your husband the demands. Get Saunders out."

That made no sense. Saunders was supposed to be the one who threatened Payton. "Why does Payton want Saunders free, he threatened to destroy Payton's car?"

"You just never mind. All you need to do is sit tight. I did my end, I got you here. Now your husband needs to do his part and then the captives can go free."

"Alma! Alma, come back!" She heard nothing over the wind beyond her prison door. If Alma was still out there, she wasn't answering. At least Elias knew where she was. He would come and free her. She wouldn't be trapped long if her big, strong husband, who protected her, knew she was there. Daisy backed into her corner and tried not to shake. The dark had never bothered her, but the shed was so small, shadowy, and cold.

Her body trembled, and she closed her eyes. "Elias, where are you?"

The latch opened, and the door swung out as Alma came flying in. "That'll teach you not to cross me. Martin will pay for your nosing around."

Alma rushed for the door, but it slammed shut. "No supper for either of you." Mr. Payton's loud laughter grew fainter as he walked away.

Daisy stayed in her corner. Alma had tricked her. It was her fault she was even there instead of at home with her husband, talking by a warm fire, with Patches in her lap.

"I suppose you're angry with me." Alma stood by the door but there was no way she could tell where Daisy was.

"Saunders would eventually get out, so your husband would be freed. You didn't have to get me involved, you could've talked to the sheriff. If you knew Payton had your husband, why didn't you tell Sheriff Spanner?"

Alma followed her voice and slid down the wall next to her. "He's had Martin for so many days, Daisy. I'm worried about him. Martin found out that Saunders and Payton were mining on someone else's land. They thought it was all dried up, but Saunders found silver and made the mistake of bragging to Payton about it. Martin didn't think it was right. He threatened Payton, told him he'd tell the owners. Saunders didn't take too kindly to Payton threatening his cousin, so he and Martin did something to Payton's auto. I don't know what. I know nothing about those things."

Daisy shook her head and tried to follow along. "So,

Saunders is in jail for threatening to do something he already did?"

"Yes. Payton was angry and had him arrested. It also kept Saunders away from the spring where the silver is, so Payton can mine as much as he wants without sharing. Payton has Martin somewhere. Either in one of these sheds or in his house. I hope he's fed Martin ... or there won't be much left of him after so long." She sniffled. "That's why I got you involved. Payton wants Saunders out now, that's why he told the police it was just a threat. I keep hoping they'll just drop the charges and set him free."

If Payton was mining all he could, Saunders would be better left in jail. "So, why does he want Saunders free?"

"Payton hasn't found anything for days. He wants Saunders to divine with his hickory rod and see if he can find any more."

Daisy rolled her eyes; thankful Alma couldn't see in the dark. There were some who believed in divining rods, but she wasn't one of them. "Those creeks have been considered clean for almost thirty years. What little they found is probably all there is."

"All this over a few flakes of silver." Alma's cold hand touched hers. "I'm so sorry, Daisy. But I did try to make Mr. Laury powerful mad so he would come right out here. I hope he hurries."

"I hope he brings the sheriff. Mr. Payton needs to go to jail for a very long time."

Alma huddled closer. "Let's just hope we don't have to stay here all night. It's cold, feels like rain coming on."

Daisy closed her eyes and prayed Elias would come before the rain.

AFTER TWO DAYS, Elias almost felt sorry for Patches. She moped around the house, howling mournfully. He wanted to howl, too. His parents would be driving in some time that day and Daisy still hadn't come back. She didn't have her trunk, her cat, not even her hair brush. Was Mr. Payton so wealthy that he could replace everything? Yet, it made no sense, Daisy wouldn't leave her cat behind. Even if she was afraid to face him, she still would, just to get her cat.

Elias stared at his hat for a moment, hanging on the wall, then slapped it on his head. He'd avoided the court-house, to give Daisy her space. But enough was enough. She needed to come get her things and he could speak to the judge about drawing up an annulment. He started his car and raced it down the street. The car protested the treatment and sputtered but sprang forward as he pressed the gas pedal.

Though he wasn't prone to fast or dangerous driving, nothing mattered anymore. He'd worked to earn his degree for Daisy, to provide a home and good life for her, he'd come all the way from Boston for Daisy, even his car had been purchased so that she would be comfortable. He'd wanted her to have what not every woman did, a man who owned a car. In the end, it hadn't mattered. Of all the things he'd worked for, she wanted the one thing Payton could give her instead. The anger clawed at him as he swerved into a spot in front of the courthouse.

His long strides ate up the distance as he made his way to her desk. He stopped, taken aback in front of her small work area. Every last thing was just where he'd put it when he'd tidied it two days before. He opened her steno case and the same roll he'd tucked inside was still there, just as he'd left it.

"Mr. Laury." Judge Cornwall's booming voice startled him. He stood in his doorway across the hall from her office. "My court reporter hasn't been in to work. I've had to call the nearest newspaper and have them send me a typist. It's not the same, but it's the best I could do on short notice. Even my backup, Mrs. Potters, isn't here. Care to tell me where your wife is, and why I shouldn't fire her?"

She hadn't come to work, hadn't come home for her cat, and the last one to have seen her was now also missing, and he'd been at home, angry with her. His heart clenched hard in his chest. "Sir, I think she's gone missing."

"You ... *think?* Mr. Laury, is she, or is she not?"

All his anger balled into a tight knot in his stomach. He'd harbored all sorts of angry thoughts toward his wife, thoughts Alma had fostered with her insinuations, but was it possible she'd only been kindling frustrations ... or outright lies?

"I haven't seen her since the noon meal, three days past."

The judge stared at him, his crystalline old eyes as hard

as granite. "Your wife has been missing for two and a half days and you didn't feel the need to tell anyone?"

He was a horrible husband. He didn't deserve her. The judge was right to censure him. "I was told that she'd taken up with Mr. Payton. When she didn't come to get her things, I came to confront her. That's when I saw that her desk hadn't changed since I was here last."

"So, if she's missing, we need to find her. I'll get Sheriff Spanner on the horn and get him up here."

The judge turned to head to his office and Elias followed. "I may have also have been the last person to see Alma Potters. She was here when I came to pick up Daisy two days ago. She's the one who told me Daisy was with Mr. Payton."

"I'm getting mighty tired of this Payton fellow. I think it's about time Sheriff Spanner goes out there and finds out what he knows.

"Alma's husband is missing too, and since Martin and Saunders are the closest cousins I've ever seen, we should probably ask Payton about Martin Potters, too."

Judge Cornwall scratched his chin. "How can so many people be missing? Custer isn't that big."

It was big enough. The judge went over to the wall and dialed the operator, asking to be connected with Sheriff Spanner, once the connection was made, the talk was short. The sheriff was on his way.

Elias's knee bounced as he sat in the leather chair, waiting for the sheriff. Daisy was somewhere out there and, now that he knew she was missing, he couldn't take action fast enough.

"You antsy?" The judge leaned back in his seat. "Justice always takes time."

"What if Daisy doesn't have time? I wasted two days." He gripped his fingers, cracking his knuckles to relieve the pressure.

The sheriff strode in and was soon up to date on all the missing people.

"I'll go out and check at the Payton place. He hasn't been home much lately, but I'll drive through."

The sheriff's uncaring attitude did little to loosen the tension knotting Elias's muscles. "Drive through? What do you hope to learn? Do you think they are tied in his front yard, waiting for you to just pick them up?"

"You know the law, Laury. I can't nose around on someone's property without a warrant."

Judge Cornwall laughed. "Well, it isn't like you're sitting in a room with a judge who just heard all the evidence." He opened a lower desk drawer and pulled out a sheet of paper. "This warrant is good for today only. You get in, find those missing people, and get out. If they are there, that will be enough to arrest him on charges of kidnapping. We can find out why later."

Elias stood and shoved his hat back on his head. "I'm coming with you."

Sheriff Spanner laughed. "You think you're a deputy now? You've got no business being there."

"My wife is missing. I'm coming."

They stood toe to toe for a minute, neither backing down, though Elias had him in height by over four inches.

"Fine. But you stay out of the house. You can roam around the grounds. That's it."

He sighed but held his tongue. It wasn't what he wanted, but at least if they found Daisy, he'd be there to tell her he was sorry.

CHAPTER 21

The hunger had abated after the first whole day, but the thirst never did. Daisy leaned against the wall, forcing her mouth to stay closed so she wouldn't lose any precious moisture. She'd prayed that it wouldn't rain, and it hadn't. Now, she wished she'd kept the thought to herself.

Elias hadn't come. She'd been so sure he would. So sure that he cared. He knew where she was, so why hadn't he? She'd tried asking Alma, but she was in worse shape than Daisy. She hadn't said a word in a whole day. Light peeked in through the cracks of the shed, but there was no hope of reaching out, beyond the slivers of light. Payton had forgotten them, hadn't come back since shoving Alma in their prison.

Sleep crept up on her, but she fought to stay awake. If she let sleep take her, she feared she may not wake up again. Her head throbbed fit to churn her stomach and if she'd had anything in it, it wouldn't be for long. Her muscles spasmed, and even shifting position sent pain through her. Alma slid one leg and groaned next to her.

"Water..." Alma's parched throat scratched out the word.

"Pray for rain." Daisy wouldn't say more, just speaking hurt, but nothing could compare to the ache in her heart. How could the man she loved, the man who'd crossed a continent to keep her from being alone, leave her there to die? But even more pressing, how had she never told him how she really felt? She'd pushed her affection on him, trying to *show* him her feelings without saying a word, but she'd never uttered them. And now she might not get the chance.

She watched the slivers of light from the cracks in the wall slowly creep across the floor. Another day was coming to a close. How many more would she see?

A loud bang and rumble made her jump and peer though the nearest knothole. It took four blinks to get enough moisture to her eyes so she could focus on the smoking car. Mr. Payton was leaving, again. This time, a slumped figure sat next to him on the seat.

Daisy pushed against Alma's hip to rouse her, but her companion didn't budge from her spot on the floor. She didn't know Martin Potters well enough to know if it was him with Payton or someone else.

"Alma, get up. It might be Martin." She shoved against Alma again, but there was no response. Alma's breathing was infrequent and shallow. Alma hadn't been taking care of herself for days prior to being locked in the shed, since she'd been so worried about Martin. She wouldn't last another two days. Part of her prayed *she* wouldn't, either.

Her eyelids drooped and then closed. She was back under the tree, sitting in the shade, reading one of her sister's romance novels in the front of the Deadwood school. Elias was still inside. She'd glanced up every time she heard the squeaking door when someone came out, and he hadn't yet. No one knew what he did alone with the teacher so long after class, but no one probably cared, besides her. He wasn't popular because he was tall, gangly, and smart. He was destined for higher learning, not farming.

He strode out of the school, his long legs were lean in well-tailored trousers, and he waited at the top of the steps. His gaze fixed on her for a moment and she tried to give him a welcoming smile before he broke the feeble contact. He took the whole schoolyard in with a sweeping glance, then descended the stairs, aimed right for her. She held her breath. Some days he visited her, others he didn't. She prayed today would be one of those days.

When he reached the ground, she tucked her feet tighter under her to make sure her skirts were straight. He stopped, just a few feet from her knees and she craned her neck to look up at him. In the sun, his hair was sandy, with lighter streaks of gold, and the faintest hint of facial hair had just begun to shadow his young jaw.

"Is this side of the tree taken?" He gestured to her right.

Her throat couldn't be trusted to form words, so she

shook her head and moved over just a bit. He sat and leaned against the tree, a few inches from her shoulder, if she wasn't so terribly frightened that he would leave, she'd lean over just a fraction of an inch and touch shoulders with him.

"My parents got a letter back from Harvard. It's all decided. That's where I'll go. I expect it to be a lot of work."

Daisy cleared her throat and prayed her voice wouldn't croak. "I would expect training to be a lawyer *would* be a lot of work. No matter where you go."

"I wish I didn't have to leave. I'd rather stay close to home." He glanced over his tall shoulder at her, his warm brown eyes melting something deep within her. "I don't know anyone there."

She didn't want him to, but she suspected he wouldn't be alone for long. He was too smart, too handsome, to stay alone. "I'm sure at Harvard there will be plenty of well-read people to keep you thinking." She slid her dime novel away from him to lay it on the ground where he couldn't see it. She'd never been embarrassed of them before, but with the knowledge of the education he would get, they felt silly.

"I have just enough well-read people to talk to here in Deadwood."

If it had been anyone else, they may have smiled. But Elias never did. His eyes grew intense and he stood, leaving her alone until Beau could pick her up.

The scene faded and a moment later, she was back under the tree, but a month had passed. Elias sat next to her and a few bumble bees set a calming hum a few feet away in the lilac bush. The hot sun of a baking spring day beat down on them. Elias touched his thumb to her palm and the tip of his finger to the dorsal side. He'd done it twice, and it was the closest he came to holding her hand. She'd agreed to marry him the week before, but only if he didn't find a wife while he was gone at school.

"Last day of school." He squeezed her hand for a moment, then let go. "Graduation is tomorrow. Then I leave. I may not see you again for a long time."

She shook her head. "You may *never* see me again. You could find the perfect woman while you're gone. I would be surprised if you didn't."

He didn't say a word, but he had to know that there would be more women in Boston than there were in Deadwood. Better choices than quiet Daisy Arnsby.

"I'll never forget you, Daisy." He picked up her hand and quickly kissed her knuckles, sending her heart into a racket, then he dashed off toward home.

ELIAS BUMPED along the city streets in his auto, following the two police officers to Mr. Payton's. According to Sheriff Spanner, Mr. Payton lived on the outside of town on a large lot that spanned about two acres. The police carriage in front pulled in and he followed down the long drive. Mr. Payton had about ten sheds and out buildings that he could see, and those would be his to check.

The two officers got out and headed to the door to knock and announce the warrant. As soon as Elias turned off his car, he ignored them. He didn't care what they did, as long as they let him know if they found Daisy. He'd asked for a doctor to be present, but they hadn't agreed, citing it would take too long to round one up. He couldn't fight that logic.

The sheds all sat in a random array around the rear of the property, as if some past owner had filled one and built the next wherever he dropped the lumber. All were chipped and had been white at some point in history. They were roughly four feet by six, with one door and no windows. Each was about five feet tall. He started with the first. It was too quiet to call out. His voice would be startlingly loud, and he wanted to be able to hear the officers, in case they yelled for him. If he was outside screaming his head off, he wouldn't hear. More likely than not, they would find Daisy and Alma in the house.

Even though the judge had suggested they avoid looking for clues, that was his aim. What else could he expect to find in the land around the house except graves. He shuddered and said another prayer for Daisy. Had he ever told her that he'd loved her? Had he admitted that he'd loved her since the very beginning? That if she'd have asked him to stay in Deadwood that long-ago spring day, he'd have thrown off his parents' wishes and stayed. He'd put too much stock in quiet Daisy's voice, but she hadn't yet found it then. If they didn't find her soon, he might never hear her voice again.

The first shed held nothing. He'd never seen an old shed that was completely empty before and he sat examining it for a moment, wondering what purpose Payton could have for so many sheds if they had nothing within them? He moved on to the next and the next, each one empty.

By the fifth one, he was frustrated. Payton wasn't hiding anything out there and the officers were still inside the house. They hadn't found anything either or hadn't let him know if they had. He pushed on to the next shed and flung the door wide. There, on the floor, lay Alma. Behind her, his precious Daisy sat slumped against the wall. She was filthy, with streaks of dirt down her face. She lay propped against Alma's hip, her mouth slack. He rushed to her as he yelled something he hoped would bring the officers.

Her eyes fluttered open and she blinked but didn't focus on him. Had Payton done something to her eyes?

"Daisy?" He knelt down next to her.

Her mouth opened, but no sound broke from her dry, cracked lips. He pulled her close, cradling her to his chest. Praise God, she was alive. He held onto Daisy as he checked Alma's wrist from where it lay on her hip. Her skin was burning hot, and her pulse was weak, but she was alive.

"I'm here. I've got you," Elias whispered to Daisy as he held her close.

One of the officers ducked in the door and gently lay Alma on her back, checking her vitals.

189

"We've got to get this one to the hospital." The officer glanced up at him. "How about that one?"

Daisy clutched the front of his jacket, her unfocused eyes glancing all around him as if she were trying desperately to see.

"I'll take her home and watch her. If she needs, I'll bring her in to see a doctor. You can come by and talk to us in a few days."

The officer nodded and carried Alma out of the shed. Daisy hadn't made a move to stand and he wasn't even certain she could.

"Didn't he give you anything? Food, water?" He pushed the clumps of dirty hair out of her eyes.

Daisy shook her head slowly. Her body shuddered and the muscles in her legs visibly convulsed and quivered. He lifted her as gently as he could and carried her back to his car. At least two and a half days without water. Not fatal, but she would need hydration. A bath would be a good start, with slow and steady rations of water. He'd take care of her, he owed her that much.

Elias clutched her closer. "I'm so sorry for believing the lies. I..." He didn't know what else to say. There would be time later for *I love you* when he'd sufficiently made up for his mistake. For now, 'I'm sorry' would have to be good enough.

He set her in the seat of his car and wished there was some way to secure her. She'd have to lean against him once he climbed in. The officers were already gone and nothing else on the property had been disturbed. Mr. Payton and Martin Potters were still missing.

As he climbed in, Daisy leaned against him, clutching his arm.

"Can't believe you're here," she whispered, so softly he had to lean in to hear her.

"Yes, I'm here, darling. I'm finally here."

Now, he needed to get her home, and nurse her back to health, along with caring for his parents, who could arrive any time. He wouldn't burden her with that right now. All he wanted was to get her back to his house, with him, where she belonged.

CHAPTER 22

Gracie bounced about underfoot as Elias tried to maneuver Daisy into the house. The neighbors had all come out to stare as he'd walked up to the house, carrying Daisy as best he could, but none had offered to help. Probably best that way as he wasn't sure what he was going to do now. He lay Daisy on the bed. Her eyes were closed. He'd need to get some liquid in her. Her body would absorb some of it in a bath, and she needed one to rid her of the filth from the shed, anyway. But how could he manage that? He didn't know any other women in Custer, except his new housekeeper, and she wouldn't be along for hours.

He left his bride to go fill the tub. Even though he had pump water to the kitchen and a water closet in the lavatory, he didn't have water to the tub. He first moved the kitchen rug near the stove, so he wouldn't have to port the water far, then he set to heating enough water in the big copper boiler that Daisy used to wash clothes. It would take a long time for all that water to get to boiling, so he used that time to add cold water to the tub first.

When he got the tub half-full, he went back to check on Daisy. She hadn't moved, and he knelt by their bed. He'd never taken advantage of a woman, and knew she needed his care, but he couldn't help feeling like he was doing something he shouldn't. He gripped her hand and pulled her knuckles against his forehead.

"Daisy, I hope you can forgive me. I'm so sorry. I never should've believed that you would ever willingly go with Payton, not after he scared you so terribly. I was weak, weak in my belief in you. I was weak in my belief in myself to be an adequate husband to you. I want to be more, I want to be a man you can be proud of. A husband you would never want to leave."

His voice left him, and his chest ached as the first tears of his adult life choked him. "I love you, Daisy."

She squeezed his hand and he glanced up to find her sweet blue eyes on him. She had no voice, but mouthed the words, "I love you, too."

He raised and sat on the bed. "I've got a bath ready for you out in the kitchen. Do you think you can walk?" He prayed she could. If he had to help her with her bath, he'd be lost.

Her eyes sought his and she shook her head. Her mouth opened to speak, and she clutched her throat. "I trust you," came the weak rasp of a voice too dry to speak.

He lifted her off the bed and prayed, like he never had

before, for the strength to do what he had to. She was his wife, he reminded himself. Very few other married men went a week and a half after being married without laying eyes on their wife, but his situation was not common. At least, not as common as it once was.

After he lifted her gently from the bed and made it down the hall to the kitchen, he felt exposed. Anyone could come to the door and see his wife, bathing in front of the stove. He hadn't considered that fact when he'd filled the tin plunge bath. He set Daisy down on a kitchen chair and knelt before her. Starting with her bodice, his hands trembled as he freed the buttons down the front and slid it off her shoulders. It had been a beautiful bright white with ruffles down the front, giving her the appearance of a tiny waist and wider shoulders than she really had.

He reached around her, unsnapping the two metal snap closures on her skirt. Lifting her slightly, he pulled the fabric out from beneath her, leaving her in her stays, and what appeared to be all one piece of chemise and drawers. Daisy held fast to the edge of the seat, chin to her chest to hold herself upright in the chair.

When they had stayed at her room in the boarding house, she'd unfastened her stays from the front, but if he did that, he'd touch her more intimately than he intended. There was only one way around that. It might be more difficult, but he wouldn't force her to endure his touch. He stood and untied the back of her stays, gently loosening it first from the waist to the top, then from the waist to the bottom, each set of strings being independent and tight. He'd restring it if he had to, but at least it would be off.

Then she sat there in front of him in just the very thin fabric of her underthings. How he wished he'd listened to Daisy. He didn't want the first time he saw his bride to be when she couldn't respond. How utterly unfair and embarrassing for her. Daisy took a deep breath and peeled her undergarments down to her waist. She reached for him and he held his breath as he helped her stand. They slid the remainder all the way to the floor. He kept his eyes averted, but it was the biggest test of will he'd ever had.

It was only two steps to the tub and Daisy made a valiant effort to walk, but he had to help her into the bath when she got there. As she lay back in the warm water, he went for a glass, so she could drink while she soaked. The tub was a nicer one that curved up at the head, supporting her back, so she was able to relax without fear of falling in. It was six feet long, so when she was ready, she could submerge, though he suspected he would be washing her hair. She just didn't have the strength.

He brought the cup to her lips and she slowly drank about half of it, then rested her head again. After he'd washed her up, trying to remain as detached as he could, Daisy grasped his hand. He stopped what he was doing, terrified that once she could make any noise, she would be furious with him.

Her voice still hadn't returned to normal, but the husky, scratchy sound was still music to his ears. "Elias, I love you, too."

∼

AFTER SOAKING in the bath until she shivered and drinking more water than she thought she could ever consume, Daisy laid her head back against the rim of the tub. Elias knelt behind her and massaged soap into her scalp, he'd warmed more water and was letting it cool to rinse the soap from her hair. His fingers gently rubbed, sending a pleasant quiver from her neck to her toes.

She knew she should be embarrassed, laying there in front of her husband who had yet to lay an intimate hand on her, but she didn't. He *was* her husband and she desired him. It wasn't wrong to do so. He gently eased her forward in the tub and she tipped her head back. He poured the warm water over her slowly, directing it so that it did the most good.

"Are you feeling better? Are you strengthened enough to try to walk back to our room?"

While her mind was finally clearing of all the muddled thoughts and her throat felt less like broken glass and closer to scratchy, she wasn't at all sure she could make it all the way back to their room on her cramping, wobbly legs. But, she also didn't want to force Elias to touch her if he didn't want to. He'd bathed her with the efficiency of a nurse, detached from the job, then let her just soak in the tub for an hour. After she'd rested, he'd washed her hair. It was foolish to be disappointed. Even if he'd excited her, she couldn't have enjoyed it, but she *was* disappointed all the same. Elias was a good man, too good, and he still didn't want to hurt her.

She did her best to push herself out of the tub, but her thick blood from her long lack of water sent vicious spasms down her legs and she slipped back down under the water with a small cry.

Elias was there in a moment with a towel. He slid his hands under her arms and hoisted her out and onto the rug, waited until she caught her balance, then wrapped her in the towel. Faster than she could think, he lifted her in his strong and capable arms and carried her back to their room.

He'd been so stoic, like a stranger, and it hurt her pride. Was she so very plain that even in her current state, he was unaffected by her? Hadn't he said he loved her? Slowly, so very gently, he laid her on their bed. He moved around behind her, sat on the mattress and gathered her wet hair out from underneath her. As he brushed each snarl, soft tingles of awareness fired from her head to her heart. He was loving her in the only way he would allow himself. She wanted to cry at his tender ministrations, but the tears would not come.

When he'd finished meticulously freeing her hair from all the knots, he braided it in a thick plait and tied one of her ribbons around the end, then leaned forward and left the gentlest kiss behind her ear.

"Lay here and rest. I'll go clean up everything in the kitchen. Mrs. Marks has been coming for the last two days and she makes supper and tidies the house for a few hours in the evening. She'll be coming in about an hour. I'll keep her out of this room, so you can rest. I put a bell by the bed, so you wouldn't have to yell. Just ring it if you need me." He kissed her once again, then draped a blanket over her and left.

There was still too much to say, and not enough voice to say it, but at least she'd managed the important bit. She'd told him of her love, but he'd also told her of his. There was hope for a real marriage, because there was love. Strange that a husband should court his wife after they were wed, but that's exactly what had happened. They had married, courted, and then loved.

She snuggled into the pillow, her head still sensitive to every touch after Elias's tender care. It didn't even matter that she was laying in their bed without a stitch on. She was home, and where she belonged. Her last thoughts in the shed had been of Elias back in school. He'd promised to never forget her, and he hadn't, he'd remembered her.

She heard a faint knock on the front door and Elias's exuberant welcome. His parents were there. Suddenly, laying abed without her under clothes on, seemed quite impractical. His parents certainly wouldn't come back to their bedroom, but it was enough to make her heart race.

"Mom! You can't go back there!" Elias yelled as the door slammed open and a petite woman with the same sandy hair and chocolate eyes as Elias burst through the doorway.

Her eyes danced with mirth as she shut the door

behind her. "I somehow knew his new bride would be you."

"How?" Daisy didn't move. She was still under the covers and towel; his mother might not see if she didn't disturb the blanket.

"He used to talk about you all the time. Daisy Arnsby. You had his heart from the fifth grade." She clucked her tongue. "Well, Elias said you'd had an ordeal and he just sent you to bed, but we drove so far, I just had to make sure it was you. You rest now, and I'll help him get the kitchen all back to rights. We'll have a good talk when you're feeling up to it."

"Can you ask Elias to send a telegram to Beau and Ruby? I didn't get a chance to." She was suddenly exhausted, but the arrival of Mr. And Mrs. Laury reminded her she'd never made it to the post.

"I'll do that, dear. Rest now. We'll have a nice long talk in the morning."

CHAPTER 23

The next day, Elias's mother, Margaret, set a tray of hot soup and a tall glass of water over Daisy's lap. The creamy broth with big chunks of potato and the golden thread of melted butter made Daisy's stomach rumble. She'd been so focused on water that she'd forgotten how hungry she was.

After his mother left the room the day before, Elias had come in and helped her put on a night dress, and that was how she remained.

"You seem to be getting your strength back quickly. I'm glad to see it." Margaret sat on a chair next to the bed and regarded her. There was reservation in her eyes that hadn't been there when she'd visited the day before.

"Yes, I'm feeling better. Elias took good care of me." She felt like a child to say such a thing, but he had.

"Did he? Well, that's good at least." Margaret took a lengthy breath and paused. "I pride myself on being a forthright woman, Daisy. Daryl and I slept upstairs last night, across from the room where your cat sleeps." Her eyebrows rose. "Now, aside from the fact that I question why you need a bedroom for a cat... Why is *your* trunk upstairs?"

The soup lost all its lovely fragrance in the span of a moment. She stirred it around, biding time, thinking of what to say that would be honest, yet not hurt her husband. Elias had said that his mother would understand, would even explain to her the need to stay apart, so why would his mother find it so odd that she wasn't in the same room as her son?

"I am there because that is where Elias would like me to be, and I've come to agree with him." At lease in words, not in her heart.

Margaret leaned forward and closed her eyes. "Why on earth would he do that? You are a married couple. It defies one of the whole reasons for being married, which is to keep you from lusts of the flesh."

Daisy bit her lip. If she told Elias's mother why, she would expose his hurt that he hadn't even wanted to share with Daisy. It was only when she was so torn by his rebuff that he'd shared his fears with her.

"He told me the story of his birth."

Margaret sighed, and her head slumped down. "He still holds that against me? I suppose he would. Heaven knows, I tried to convince him of the truth, but he wouldn't hear it. After he was born, there was a problem with the afterbirth. It bled more than it should, and I almost died from the loss. Somewhere along the way, he got it in his head that it was his fault."

"He thinks it's because he's so big."

She laughed, but her eyes were laced with tears. "My lovely son was no bigger than an average baby. He grew quickly as a toddler, but we knew he would. You haven't seen his father yet, but they both have to duck through doorways, and then some."

"But, what about his grandmother? He said she almost died, too."

Margaret bit her lip. "Elias's grandmother was a wonderful woman, loved him to distraction, but she was a mail-order bride. You see, most men in 1836 didn't reach six feet tall. There was no one in Independence who would go anywhere near him, when he was ready to wed. So, he sent off for a bride. When she arrived from out of state, she was shocked, but stuck. She agreed to have one child for him to pass along his line and that was it. I don't know what she would've done if she'd have sprouted a girl, but lucky for her, Daryl was born."

Daisy's heart ached for Elias. He'd lived his whole life believing a lie that had shaped who he was, not on the outside, as he thought, but on the inside. That lie had forced him into asking a plain young woman to wait for him, one who *wasn't* all that he deserved, because he didn't think he was worthy of anyone else.

"He married me out of fear." As much as she tried, she couldn't hold back the tears. "If he knew the truth, really knew it, I wouldn't have been his choice. He is handsome, smart, successful. Any woman would be so blessed to call him hers. But he believed a lie, believed he didn't deserve any better than me. And now he can never be free." Daisy handed the tray back to Margaret, almost untouched, and rolled over to hide her tears.

"You need to tell him, make him understand," Daisy said.

"I've tried, dear. It's obvious he doesn't believe me."

"He thinks you sleep apart."

Margaret laughed, the sound grating to Daisy's ears. "We do, but only because Daryl is so big and barrel chested that when he snores, they can hear it in the next county. I have to sleep in another room just to get some rest. It isn't that I want to, and it isn't that he wants me to. It also isn't all the time."

"Tell him."

Margaret laid a gentle hand on Daisy's hip and turned her on her back to look Daisy in the eyes.

"I will speak to him, but this is something you both will need to discuss. You're a married couple now. It's up to you to work out the intimate nature of your relationship. That is one place no one else has any business."

Daisy nodded but hated the thought of bringing it up, yet again. Margaret's footfalls clicked down the short hall. Elias didn't feel what she did. He couldn't. She was tempted by him with just a glance. Yet bathing, brushing her hair, and dressing her had done nothing. He hadn't even touched her last night, choosing to lay on top of the coverlet again with space between them, back to the way they'd been the first night she'd slept in his bed.

They may never speak of it. When Margaret told him the truth, and allayed his fears, he may have some deep regrets. He might want an annulment. Daisy clutched her knees and wrapped herself in a protective ball. Patches jumped up on the bed and curled in for some attention, and Daisy couldn't even reach out to her precious friend.

Down the hall, Elias spat, "I don't want to hear this!" The door slammed. All went silent, and Daisy's heart broke.

ELIAS SLID into Sheriff Spanner's hard seated wagon and held on as they rushed through the town and over to the jail. The sheriff hadn't said much, just that Mr. Saunders wanted to see him and that it was urgent. Being the man's lawyer, he couldn't ignore it, even though he would rather stay home and make sure his wife rested and his mother did her job. Which is why he'd lost his temper when the officer had shown up.

The interior of the jail house was dark. It didn't seem to matter that the lamps were on, the cement seemed to eat every ray it cast. A jail was no place for laughter or light. Saunders sat at the table where he always met Elias, but his usual bluster was gone. He hid his head in his shackled hands. Elias sat across from him and waited to hear what was so important that he'd get a summons.

"He's dead. That bastard killed Martin." Harvey's voice came from somewhere deep within. Strong, even though his hands muffled the sound.

"How do you know?" He wasn't ready to feel anything, not until he was sure this wasn't another ploy. Saunders was good at twisting the truth.

"Deputy came in to tell me about an hour ago. They got word that someone was trespassing at the place on French Creek. They went to see if they could catch the man in the act. They did. It was Payton, trying to bury Martin."

And he'd have been digging another for Daisy in a few days if he hadn't found her. "Why don't you tell me the whole story? I suspect that I'll be defending you against more than a threat of destruction of property in the near future."

"I never agreed to killing."

He lifted his head, then let it fall into his palms again. "I found silver flakes out at the Houseman place. It has the easiest access to the creek and I was going to walk upstream to go fishing. There's never anyone around, so I didn't figure they'd mind. Something in the riverbed glinted back at me a little. I thought it was just the sun on the water for a minute, but when I scooped it up in my hand and scratched at it with my knife ... I knew."

Harvey's shoulders hunched. "That's where it should've stopped. I wish I could say it did, but I was greedy. One night at the saloon, I told Payton I would be rich and didn't even have to buy the land first. He followed me one day and told me that if I didn't let him take his share, he'd report my theft. Martin knew, but he didn't want anything to do with it. He thought it was stealing. Martin's always been a little simple and it wasn't like we were looking for the vein … just the broken remains that were in the river…"

Saunders sighed heavily. "He didn't deserve to die for defending me. Martin wanted our panning to stop, so he put something in Payton's auto, bacon fat or something. Smoked to beat all. Payton was furious. He thought it was me, trying to make sure that he couldn't search for more rocks. So, he reported me and here I sit."

Elias waited. There was more to the story, but how much did Saunders really know? He'd been in jail for almost two weeks.

"He sent me notes, but I think Payton either got hold of one or discovered Martin. He'd been hiding in Payton's yard. Payton came in here and told me he had Martin and he'd free him when I got out to keep an eye on my wayward cousin. He needed me to find more silver. The bed ran dry. He was regretting having me arrested, and I was happy to stay to keep him angry."

"That's why you told me I needed to get you out, you finally decided you cared when he had your cousin. Why didn't you work harder for a compromise, knowing your cousin was being held by Payton?" That was the only piece he couldn't place. Saunders had wanted out, but hadn't seemed in that much of a hurry, telling him he got good food and quiet. Elias hadn't rushed, nor really worked toward a good compromise, since Saunders hadn't been willing.

Saunders sighed and hunched his shoulders. "You've seen Payton. Would you ever think that man, that dandy, scrawny, man was capable of murder? He brought *waders* to the river so his pants wouldn't get wet. He's a lazy, rich fool. I never thought he'd kill Martin, never even thought he'd hurt him, so I didn't try to get out fast, since that's what Payton wanted, and I was sore he'd put me in here in the first place."

Payton had presented as a weak foe, though he'd caught a hint of the underlying evil, Elias still hadn't thought of him as anything more than competition for Daisy. He'd never thought Payton was capable of hurting anyone, until Elias had pulled Daisy out of that shed himself.

"I see Payton isn't here. Where are they keeping him?" Elias asked.

"No one's saying. They don't want him near me and I was here first. He's the first murderer Custer has seen in a long time. Might not be able to get a fair trial here."

That was true. Custer and Hill City were both quiet towns, and though Payton's methods weren't violent, the people would want to know what happened, and they would form their opinion before it ever went to trial. Finding twelve people who hadn't heard about the case would be almost impossible within a few days.

"I'll give back every rock with silver in it. I'll work like a dog for the Houseman's to pay back my debt. But I didn't kill Martin, didn't agree to anything like that. You've got to believe me."

Elias was used to the pleading. That stage always came when a client realized that, without him, they would probably be put away for a long time. He'd become hardened to it. He had to be. He'd work as hard as he could, he'd try. But he never let himself get as emotionally involved in a case as he already was on this one.

"I'll have to see what you've actually been charged with. You were in jail, so they may not charge you as an accessory. If you're a praying man, I suggest you start. Poor Alma. I don't know what she'll do."

Saunders glanced up, his eyes redder than Elias expected. The prisoner had been holding back tears for the cousin who'd been closer than a brother.

"She won't have to fuss over him anymore. Maybe she'll eventually find some peace. Tell her I'm sorry. Will you? I don't know what else to say."

It had been a little over a day since Alma had been found, and he hadn't gone to see how she was doing in the hospital. He'd been too concerned with his own bride. She'd probably already gotten a visit by an officer like Saunders had and, though she'd done nothing but sew strife in Elias's marriage, he felt sorry for her.

"I'll let her know. Don't talk to anyone else about this. You don't actually have to tell the police anything, so don't."

Elias stood and slid his chair under the table, and the scrape along the cement floor echoed through the cells.

When he'd only had to worry about himself, life had been easy. Now, he had a full day of work ahead of him and all he wanted to do was curl up with his wife and pretend the last hour hadn't happened. He'd be a part of the biggest case Custer had seen in years, and it would keep him far busier than he wanted to be.

CHAPTER 24

Margaret had insisted that Daisy remain in bed one more day, and they took the chance while Elias was out to go see the town, leaving her with a quiet house and too much to think about. His mother hadn't seemed perturbed in the slightest by his anger just prior to leaving, and she was hesitant to bring it up to ask.

When the evening sent the shadows long across her bed, she decided it was high time to get dressed and join the family for supper. Elias's father had been there for more than a whole day and she'd yet to meet him, being cooped up in her bedroom. Though Elias had said he wanted her with him before she'd been taken, the specter of a passionless marriage still hung over them.

At least he'd said he loved her, she could cherish that. She could give him her love and it would have to be enough.

As she finished her hair, a knock came, and she rushed to get it. Elias had said he'd hired a maid, but she'd yet to meet the woman and it was late in the evening for her to be just coming. Daisy opened the door to find Ruby, looking stylish in a green gored walking skirt and blouse, her red curls tucked into a tidy bun.

Daisy pulled her into an embrace. It had been years since she'd allowed herself to go home and Ruby had aged, with soft laugh lines framing her eyes.

"Where is Beau, and Joseph?" Daisy gripped her hands and drew her into the room.

Ruby smiled softly and glanced behind her. "Beau is on his way around the house. He rented a buggy for us at the livery and he's putting it away in that old stable behind the house."

"Oh, I don't even think there's feed in there or anything." Daisy wasn't sure what to do about it, though Beau would know how to take care of horses. She hadn't since she'd left Deadwood.

"I'm sure he'll manage." Ruby rested her hand gently on Daisy's shoulder. "It's been far too long. So long that you managed to court and wed, before we even knew about it." There was hurt in her sister's soft voice, but Ruby had always been tough. She wouldn't cry, and only those who knew her best would ever know she was bothered in the slightest.

"That's an easy enough answer. We didn't court. Elias and I made a promise to each other in school, and we kept it."

"Oh, Daisy." Ruby slumped into the nearest chair. "I wanted so much better for you. That's not so very different from our father's arrangement."

Ruby may have wanted more, but there was none better for her than Elias. It was Elias's parents who should have that feeling, not her own.

"Ruby, he is a wonderful husband. I love him with all my heart."

"Do you?" Her eyebrows drifted up, and Daisy bit back a laugh. Beau would do the same thing when he came in and asked her. Telling Ruby first gave her the strength to tell Beau, because she'd feared telling him up until then.

A second quick knock came on the door and then Beau entered, tapping his boots just outside the threshold. He smiled in his lopsided way and came forward, giving her a quick hug and kiss on the forehead. "Daisy, it was good to hear from you." He sat next to his wife and glanced up at her.

Daisy took a seat, so they could relax, and it would keep her from pacing. While it was true, she did love her husband, and he said he loved her, there was a large piece missing. Beau and Ruby, who'd loved each other for almost twenty years, might see it.

"As I was saying to Ruby... I love Elias. I may have originally married him because I promised to, but if he'd wanted to marry me on that very day so long ago, I would've also said yes ... after asking you, of course."

Beau nodded and took his wife's hand. "I met Elias many times when I picked you up from school. He seemed good enough back then, and his parents were good people."

Elias's parents had not been in the same circle as Beau and Ruby, and she was unsure how they ever would've met. "Did you meet them when you worked for the Deadwood newspaper?" It was the only connection she could make.

"No, when I saw how he hung around the school most days—whether he was sitting with you or not—watching to make sure I picked you up, I found out who he was and talked to his parents. He's a solid young man, raised well."

Daisy's heart swelled, and she wanted to jump out of her seat and hug the only father she could truly remember. "So, you approve of him? I was so worried you wouldn't."

"He had the right seeds planted in him. Good Christian parents, solid upbringing, good in school, no trouble. *If* I'd have been asked, I'd have given my blessing."

A lump formed in her throat. "And ... are you angry that I didn't?"

"I would've liked the courtesy, but I had already suspected long ago that graduation wasn't the last time I would set eyes on Elias Laury."

The front door swung open and Daisy sprang to her feet as the man himself walked through, followed by his parents. Introductions were made out of respect and both sets of parents were soon talking.

Elias slipped his arm around her and leaned in close to her ear. "Mom said we needed to have a good talk. I'm taking us out to supper, then booking a few rooms at the hotel for them, so we can have an evening alone."

Daisy met his eyes and wanted to talk with him, but her family had just come. "Don't you think it would be rude to send them away when they just arrived?" she whispered.

He squeezed her arm and smiled. "I have a suggestion." Elias waited until all four parents were silent and looking at him. "Daisy has been under the weather and is only just returning to health. Also, my table is quite small, we've had difficulty seating just the three of us. Might I interest you in supper at the hotel? I've also arranged for private rooms for you for tonight."

Margaret smiled. "That's lovely dear. You and Daisy have had so little time alone since we've been here. It will be good for you."

Beau and Ruby glanced at each other, a skeptical frown furrowing each face.

Elias piped up quickly. "I was going to wait to surprise you all with this. Daisy doesn't even know..." He took her hand and his simple glance electrified her.

"After our supper, the minister will be joining us in the gathering room at the back of the hotel for a ceremony. Daisy and I were never married in front of a proper preacher and I don't feel right about that. Beau, may I have permission to properly marry your daughter?"

Daisy gasped and gripped his hand tighter. She'd never dreamed she'd get a wedding, not a real one.

Ruby glowed up at Beau with a radiant smile, and he quirked his eyebrow.

"Took you long enough."

DAISY CLUTCHED Elias's arm as they stood before a minister she'd never met. His name didn't matter. Elias had gone out of his way to arrange a wedding for her, a real one, in front of a minister and witnesses. Her family was present. She hadn't felt loved at the first, but the way Elias glanced down at her, his eyes glowed with sincere love, this was the wedding she would remember.

She glanced over her shoulder at Beau and Ruby and warmth filled her heart. The minister read a few passages, then glanced up at them and smiled.

"I know that you both have been married for almost two weeks, according to the State of South Dakota, but a covenant is precious in the sight of the Lord. This ring," he held up a gold band that Daisy hadn't realized he had, "symbolizes to the world, that you are together, unbreakable. Elias, place this ring on your bride's finger as a testament to the world that you are one flesh, one body, with you as the head. Just as we are all one body of Christ, with the Lord Jesus as the head."

Elias, with shaky fingers, slid the cool ring on her finger. Though she'd legally been his before the ceremony, she now felt like he was her husband before God. Elias leaned forward and gently brushed his lips over hers. Like everything else that night, though it was an action he'd done before, it felt new, exciting, thrilling.

They shook hands with the minister and he left shortly thereafter. Elias led them to a large table that the hotel had set aside just for them. The conversation was light as they reminisced about Deadwood and all the changes over the last twenty years, how the world had changed.

Beau smiled and took Ruby's hand, then glanced around the table. "Ruby and I have been talking. Aiden and Hugh have the Ferguson place well in hand. They don't need me anymore, probably haven't for years. Joseph is almost a man now and Barton has offered to take him on over in Belle Fourche."

Daisy's head swam. Before Beau and Ruby were married, Beau suffered from terrible wanderlust. "What do you have planned?"

Ruby beamed. "We don't know where we'll go. But we stayed in South Dakota long enough to see you all married and happy. I asked that of Beau, and though it nearly killed him to stay put, he has."

He leaned over and nuzzled her ear. "Not that it's been easy."

Now that she'd seen them, it was as if she was losing them all over again. "You will write, and let us know where you go?"

Beau's smile took over his face, she hadn't seen him that happy since he became a father. "Postcards. It's the only way we can send to all of you. Wherever we go, we'll send some out. If we plan to stay anywhere long, we'll let you know."

Ruby slid forward in her chair, her eyes wide with excitement. "I'm truly looking forward to it. I've only ever seen the area around Cutter's Creek and the hills of South Dakota. I'm ready to see what this great nation has to offer."

The rest of the meal was spent chatting about the best places to go, but Daisy couldn't concentrate. Her own mother, Maeve, had left Cutter's Creek years before and gone off. She'd also said she would write, but letters became more and more rare until they stopped, and when Daisy had tried to write to her, the letter was marked return to sender. Hopefully Ruby would be better at keeping up a connection.

When they finished, Elias paid the bill and took Mr. Laury and Beau to the front desk to get the keys to their rooms.

Margaret clasped Daisy's hand. "You be sure to have that talk with him when you get home. No time like the present."

Ruby sat silently, and did not inquire, though Daisy could feel the questions in Ruby's mind by the slight tilt of her head and the set of her shoulders. She would not bring up such intimate details at the table, but Ruby need not worry.

"Elias and I need some time to catch up. All that matters, is that I'm home now and my ordeal brought Elias and I closer together."

Ruby nodded, but she was not placated. Though, of all her *children*, she only bore Joseph, Ruby had had to raise seven daughters and she could read each one as if she were their parent.

The men returned, and they shared warm, though strained goodbyes.

"I've let my client know that I'm only available tomorrow in an emergency. Tomorrow, we will spend the day together, all six of us as a family." Elias gently placed her hand around his arm and her heart did a little flip.

They would be home shortly, and again, newly married.

CHAPTER 25

They didn't talk as Elias drove home from the hotel. He had a lot to say to Daisy but didn't want to talk to her there, in the open car. Home was more intimate, more private. Though no one could hear them over the rumble of the engine, he also didn't want to have to yell what he had to say. It was for her to hear, and no one else. Though part of him did want to whoop like a boy who'd just been kissed for the first time. Because that's what he felt like.

He parked the car and came around to Daisy's side, opened the door for her and waited for her to gracefully climb down. She was a beauty, even in the moonlight. The soft breeze played with her hair and her beautiful face turned to him.

He closed her door, then lifted her in his arms, carrying her across the lawn.

"Elias, what are you doing? The neighbors!" Daisy

laughed as she hid her face in his neck. His body thrilled at the heat of her breath and the tickle of her hair against his skin.

"I'm carrying my bride across the threshold. The only time I got to do that before was after your abduction, and I'd prefer to not remember that time."

She clung to his shoulders and he held her tighter. Once they were inside, he kicked the door closed with his foot. He considered whether he should set her down, or just carry her back to the one place he would feel comfortable revealing everything to his wife. She sensed his hesitation and leaned back, looking him in the eyes.

"Elias? What's the matter?"

His heart was the matter. He'd thought all day about his mother and his original hope that she would turn Daisy's mind, but a fear had poked to the surface he hadn't wagered on. A fear that Daisy might actually listen.

He strode with purpose to their bedroom, flicked on the dim gas light, then laid Daisy down on the bed. Her blue eyes were so soft, warm, welcoming. His mother hadn't succeeded.

"I've got so much to talk to you about, but I've wanted to hold you all day." He slid his suit coat off and draped it over the chair, then his tie and vest met the same fate. Daisy propped herself on her elbow and watched him with a hunger in her eyes that he couldn't help but appreciate.

He went around the bed and slid in behind her, pulling her flush with his body and kissing her in the spot he loved, right behind her ear. Her hair was soft and smelled better than the most luxurious perfume. She sighed and leaned against him.

"Daisy, I left this morning angry, and I'm sorry. I didn't want to leave you. I promised to work hard to provide for you for the rest of our lives and I didn't want to do that today. I also promised to take care of you when we said our vows at the courthouse, but I didn't do that, either. Because of my failure, you were taken."

"But Elias—"

He covered her sweet lips with his, just long enough that he could feel her relax once again. "Darling, let me finish."

Her eyes burned even hotter. If he didn't finish his talk soon, he never would.

"That was why it was important for me to say our vows tonight, in front of witnesses and God."

"Elias, it was never you. I was taken because I didn't listen to you. We were married, but I didn't feel like your wife, and Alma needed my help, so I chose her over you. I thought you'd never know. I'm so sorry. Please forgive me."

He wasn't about to hold it against her, not when he'd been the one to foster her inaccurate feelings. He hadn't treated her like a wife. Had hoped she'd feel anything but. "I love you. I don't ever want you to doubt that again."

She rolled to face him and rubbed her cheek against his. "Your mother spoke to me this morning."

He tensed, his mother had been quicker and more efficient than he'd thought.

"She explained to me that when you were born, you

were of average size. You weren't the reason she almost died. You weren't too big then, and I'm not frightened of you now."

Her nuzzling brought their bodies flush. "My dear wife. I think it's time you were mine." He kissed her, and she buried her hands in his hair, drawing him closer to her. Within minutes, all her hairpins were lost to the pillow and her lips were plump with his kissing.

"Say the word, Daisy. I need to hear that you'll have me as your husband. Because I've never wanted anyone but you."

She drew his face gently down to her lips once more and mouthed the words against his. "I do."

CHAPTER 26

June 1915

D aisy walked down to the mailbox and flipped open the front. Four postcards waited, and she smiled as she glanced at the pictures on each one.

Beau and Ruby had left in September of 1910, for parts unknown within the United States. They'd gone back to visit Cutter's Creek first, then Oregon and California. No one had heard anything from them for months. Just when Daisy had started to worry, she'd gotten three postcards from Nevada. Now, the postcards always came in batches.

Beau and Ruby were staying in a little town named Dry Bayou, Texas, making new friends, but they would move on soon. Though they'd said they would let the family know if they planned to stay anywhere long, they never did, always on the move.

Daisy rubbed the swell of her belly, a habit that had just begun as her womb stretched her abdomen wide out in front of her. Elias was a tender and loving husband, but he'd insisted on avoiding intimacies during her most fertile times, however the Lord had other plans.

Six months before, her cycle had shifted unexpectedly. Even the doctors couldn't explain it, and she'd conceived. Her lack of a child had been a heartache she hadn't shared with anyone, not even Elias, but the Lord knew her heart and heard her cry. Now, she just needed to prove to her dear man that she wouldn't break if he looked at her wrong.

She strode back into the house and Elias sat in his favorite chair, old Gracie, gray in the muzzle, lifted her head for a moment, then laid back down when she saw who it was. Daisy smiled and sat next to her husband, handing him the postcards.

"Well, it looks like they will travel until they see every last inch of this nation. I don't know how they do it."

Daisy did. Beau was a master at adapting quickly and finding work wherever he went. "He was built to roam, and Ruby was made to follow him."

"So be it. I hope you don't mind that I would much rather stay right here." He took her hand and rubbed it gently.

"As would I, as long as I'm right here with you." The little one inside gave her a hearty kick and she rubbed her belly once again. She'd just received a letter from Hattie, whose womb had been closed for many years. She was now pregnant with her first child, as well. Hugh had decided that she wasn't to lift a finger for the entire pregnancy, no matter how simple. Hattie was near to pulling out her hair in exasperation with him, but was overjoyed.

Joseph, Beau and Ruby's son, was in Belle Fourche, and Barton, along with his brothers, was keeping him in hand. Jennie and Aiden had two children, both boys, and they stayed close to the Ferguson Ranch. Nora was the best at keeping in contact, though, they were the closest in age. She and her sheriff were happy in Hot Springs, with two children of their own. She'd started making her hats from their home after they had started a family. Her creations were in high demand.

Patches leapt onto Daisy's lap and waited for attention. Her life would change in a few months when her own baby came, but the more things changed, the better they seemed to get. South Dakota would always be her home, no matter which part she visited, because with seven sisters, her little family was always welcome in any part of the state.

ABOUT THE AUTHOR

Kari Trumbo is a writer of Christian Historical Romance and a stay-at-home mom to four vibrant children. She does freelance developmental editing and blogging. When she isn't writing or editing, she homeschools her children and pretends to keep up with them. Kari loves reading, listening to contemporary Christian music, singing with the worship team, and curling up near the wood stove when winter hits. She makes her home in central Minnesota with her husband of eighteen years, two daughters, two sons, and two cats.

Thank you, dear reader, for joining me on this adventure. I hope you've enjoyed it and that you'll continue reading the other books I have available, listed on the next page.

Be sure to join my special reader list to find out when my next novel will be released. You can also get a free book at www.KariTrumbo.com.

74712150R00142

Made in the USA
Middletown, DE
30 May 2018